FIRE
DANCER

Other Books by Catherine Jones Payne

The Broken Tides Trilogy
Breakwater
Crosscurrent
Maelstrom

The Broken Tides Stories
A Gathering Tempest
Daughter of the Rivers
To Wander the Paths of the Sea

FIRE DANCER

CATHERINE JONES PAYNE

FATHOM INK™

FIRE DANCER

Published in the United States by Fathom Ink Press.

Visit www.fathominkpress.com for more information.

ISBN (paperback)   978-1-946693-14-3
ISBN (ebook – EPUB)   978-1-946693-13-6
ISBN (ebook – MOBI)   978-1-946693-12-9

Cover Design: Jenny Zemanek, Seedlings Design Studio.
Interior Design: Chris Bell, Atthis Arts.
Ebook Formatting: Kella Campbell, E-Books Done Right.
Author Photo: Steven Noreyko.
Epigraph "Dustfire" Copyright © 2019 by Janeen Ippolito

Visit the author at www.catherinejonespayne.com

Facebook: catherinejonespayneauthor
Instagram: catherinejonespayne

For Brittany, sister extraordinaire, woman of valor,
who by her strength calls forth the strength of others.

outlasting the fire around me
I breathe out the fire within
me
and stand
and soar

on embers
dreams
and dustfire

—Janeen Ippolito - "Dustfire"

ONE

I grabbed Nolan's hand as we passed underneath the vivid floral arch that marked the entrance to the great Orivesi Terra Market. All around us, brilliant colors clamored for attention, advertising food, garments, machinery, tools—anything our hearts desired. But my attention was focused on Nolan, on his tall, lanky frame, the blond hair that fell in waves almost to his shoulders, and his brilliant green eyes that rested on me.

I broke out of my reverie to glance around and make sure no one from the clan was watching. It was probably foolish to sneak through the market with Nolan. I wouldn't make a habit of it. But I didn't see any other Fintan here. At least not right now.

My clan had set up camp just two miles from Nolan's home and planned to stay two whole months while the festival performed in the region. Nolan and I could hardly believe our good fortune. We'd schemed to see each other whenever we could since we were young children. The Fintan usually came to Orivesi twice a year, for four or five weeks at a time. But to be this close to each other for so long was something we'd only dreamed of.

He grinned at me, and the smile lit up his whole face. "What are you thinking about?"

I returned the smile. "About how much I've missed you."

"Aye," he said. "You were too long in Parkano this time."

"And Juankoski before that."

He squeezed my hand. "A year."

"Aye, almost. Ten months and sixteen days." I'd counted every one of them.

"Snail rolls!" called a dark-haired busker, moving into our path. "Only two pennies each."

Nolan dug in his pocket and pulled out a handful of coins for the busker. He picked out two snail rolls from her bag and handed one to me.

I bit into the bread, closing my eyes at the decadent taste—the lightness of the pastry, the rich custard, the sweet raisins. They were sold only here in the province of Orivesi, and I'd missed them almost as much as I'd missed Nolan when I was gone.

Almost.

"You going to chew those or just inhale them?" Nolan laughed as I stuffed a massive piece of roll into my mouth.

I shrugged. Couldn't talk around the pastry anyway.

At another stall, I spotted my friends Aislinn and Liam, holding hands. They were Fintan, but I wasn't worried about them seeing us. They wouldn't give us away. I suppressed a smile just as Liam turned and noticed me. He looked from me to Nolan and back again and shook his head.

"Be careful," he mouthed.

I rolled my eyes and waved him off. Liam worried too much. But I was glad to see him with Aislinn. He'd been sweet on my awful cousin Shayla for the longest time, and I'd begun to worry his head was addled.

Nolan tossed another penny at a young man selling flowers and selected a bouquet of simple white daisies from the myriad of options. He handed me the bouquet and then pulled one daisy free and tucked it behind my ear. "There."

My stomach fluttered. It was good to be back.

A thick, familiar scent floated on the air. Smoke.

Nolan smelled it, too, and we craned our heads, looking for the source.

"There." I pointed east. Black smoke poured up into the

sky. Never a good sign. White smoke usually meant a relatively innocuous blaze. A cooking fire, perhaps, or a small forest fire.

But black smoke often meant something besides wood was burning—like the possessions inside a house or a barn.

Nolan shook his head. "It's been too dry. There have been too many fires lately."

My stomach churned. *Too many fires?* I pushed down the horrifying implications.

"We should go help," he said.

"The quellers will put it out. They always do."

"Always good to have the fire folk in town," he murmured.

I drew back and stared at him, my brow ruffled. "You're fire folk, too, you know."

"Aye." He shrugged. "I guess I am. Just not Fintan."

I sighed and squeezed his hand. "Nay. Not yet, anyway."

I'd never met Nolan's family, and he'd never met mine. It was easier that way. At least that's what Nolan always said. And he was probably right. While it wasn't expressly forbidden for the Fintan to socialize with outsiders, it was . . . frowned upon. Nolan's papa had once been Fintan. He'd left our clan twenty years ago to marry Nolan's mama.

"You're still hoping you can somehow convince the council to let me in?" He chuckled. "Give it up, Kyla. It's hopeless. Once someone leaves, it's done. There's no way back."

"But you know the fire magic," I said. "That's got to count for something."

His countenance darkened. "Aye. It might count for an excuse for the council to move against my papa."

The Fintan High Council *would* be in a white-hot rage if they found out that Nolan's papa was teaching the magic outside of the community and raising his children to do the same. But that was why we needed to figure out a way to get them readmitted to the clan. Nolan's mama had been dead for a dozen years now, and all Nolan's siblings had the gift. There was nothing keeping them outside.

I'd find a way, eventually.

Another seller tugged at my sleeve, and I glanced at her wares and shook my head. I didn't have any need for more pottery. But something in her gaze caught me—a brokenness, or maybe hopelessness. I eyed her tattered dress and pulled three coins out of the pouch that was tied around my waist. Her face lit up when I put the coins in her hand. After holding eye contact with her a moment longer, I turned away and walked further into the crowd with Nolan, the sadness tightening my chest.

This time, my gaze roved deeper into the market. Amid the bright colors and festive atmosphere, the signs of poverty and want were stark warnings. The gaunt-eyed women in daringly low-cut dresses approaching well-dressed men with bawdy flirtation. The children—orphans, I'd been told—trying to sell their wares above the din of the market. The threadbare garments and telltale signs of illness that many of the vendors tried to mask with tight smiles.

The market was beautiful, but it always broke my heart.

But what could be done? For all my complaints about the strict rules of the Fintan High Council, my situation was better than this. We ran the best show in the land and brought in sufficient coin for our needs—and the council made sure that each clan member received an equal share of the common purse. Even the thane himself got the same allotment as the rest of us.

The earth wizards had no such central government, no rules that they all respected. They didn't live in community—they farmed, built, crafted, and sold their wares in markets like this one. But it wasn't enough to stave off poverty and desperation among them.

The Fintan clan members were kept safe from such a fate. Because of the rules.

But surely even the strictest rules ought to have exceptions? I wouldn't give up hope that, in time, Nolan's family could rejoin the clan. That he would come with me when we traveled, even into the far reaches of the continent. That somehow, we would . . .

I let the thought trail off without finishing it. I was still sixteen. A whole year away from any risk of formal betrothal. My sister Breanna hadn't been betrothed until she was nineteen, and she'd only gotten married four months ago, right after her twentieth birthday.

But Nolan had always been my best friend, and I didn't want anything to change that.

A shower of pale-pink flower petals rained down around us, and I lifted my hand to catch one. With a laugh, I blew it off my hand and watched it spin slowly toward the ground. Which earth wizard had sent the shower of petals? When my eyes found him, I handed him two pennies for his efforts.

I elbowed Nolan in the side. "What's your favorite thing you've seen so far here?"

"You. Or maybe the snail rolls. Those are pretty good too."

My stomach flip-flopped, but I rolled my eyes anyway. Though I couldn't suppress the blush I was sure had crept over my face.

I always blushed.

Breanna blamed the flame-red hair we'd inherited from Papa.

"Let's go down to the creek," I said, pulling Nolan through the crowd. "You need to teach me the magecraft you've learned this year."

"Just make sure the council doesn't find out where you learned it."

I gave a dark laugh. "The council can't know I've learned it at all. Can't possibly trust a woman with magecraft."

He shook his head. "It's absurd. You're a quicker study than anyone in my family. You'd be a great mage."

He was right, but the council wouldn't see it that way. The elemental fire had beckoned my heart from the time I was small. But, except for two or three small magecraft skills that every clan member learned, I was cut off from mastering it. Because I was a girl.

We escaped to the edge of the crowd and slipped past a couple of stalls, leaving the market. When we reached the dry, crackling grass, I stooped to remove my sandals but then thought better of it. "I'll content myself with being the Phoenix," I said. "As soon as Breanna retires."

If I can convince them to give the role to me instead of Shayla.

"Are you dancing in the troupe yet?"

I grabbed his hands and spun him around. "Aye! Eight months ago they moved me from the understudy troupe to the primary troupe. So once Breanna retires in a couple years, I'll try out for Phoenix. I've always wanted it. More than anything."

That wasn't *quite* true. Aye, I'd longed my whole life to be the principal dancer. But the last year or two I'd begun to have the sneaking suspicion that it wouldn't fully sate me. That my drive to achieve wouldn't be assuaged by landing the role.

And I wasn't sure what to do about that.

"I'm sure you'll get it," he said. "Especially if you can sneak in some subtle magecraft with the fire dancing. They'll just think you've mastered a secret dance trick."

Something about the suggestion didn't feel fair to me, but I didn't dismiss the idea entirely. Blazes, I'd need every advantage to beat my cousin. Shayla wanted to be the troupe's principal dancer as badly as I did, and since her papa was the thane, the council was likely to give it to her, even if she wasn't the best.

And if I was honest with myself, it was hard to say who *was* the best. Shayla was dazzling, with more elegance than anyone in the troupe save Breanna.

But my spins were quicker, my leaps higher. Shayla might be more graceful, but I was stronger.

We walked eastward, down a narrow path lined with stones, following the distant sound of rushing water. When we reached the trees that grew along the banks of the creek, I sank onto a rock to gaze out at the water. The creek was a little lower than normal, and my mind turned back to what Nolan had said about it being too dry. That there had been too many fires.

"Has your family been able to put out the fires?" I asked.

He shifted. "A couple of them. One burned down a storehouse. Didn't kill anyone, thank the eternal flame."

I glanced in the direction of the fire. I couldn't see any traces of it through the trees, but the smell of smoke still hung heavy in the air.

The Fintan used fire for everything, but that meant we knew how to use it with care and respect. And how to quell it.

Surely the quellers would put out this new blaze before anyone got hurt.

Shaking away my thoughts, I looked up at Nolan. "So," I said, a gleam in my eye. "Show me."

He chuckled. "You're incorrigible, you know that?"

"Always."

"Well." He sat down on the rock next to me and whispered in a conspiratorial tone, "I can make that shrub over there catch fire."

I rolled my eyes. "You taught me that three years ago."

"But it won't burn up."

That got my attention. I sat up. "I've never seen anyone do that."

"Is that a challenge?"

"It's impossible. You're teasing me."

He shook his head. His grin was insufferable now. "I'll show you."

He turned toward the shrub and held up his hands. I couldn't see his face, but I'd watched him use magecraft before. His eyes were closed, and he was probably moving his lips to form the right words. But he never said them aloud, except when he was teaching me. His papa had taught him to use magecraft silently.

Fire exploded in the shrub, the flames' red-orange tendrils pulsing around the leaves likes a living being.

I crossed my arms and stared at it, willing the branches to blacken.

But they didn't. The bush didn't burn.

I waited, counting to ten. The fire still blazed amid the branches, giving off tremendous heat, and the leaves had perhaps started to brown. But the bush hadn't caught fire.

The. Bush. Hadn't. Caught. Fire.

Nolan dropped his hands, and the fire winked out of existence.

I opened my mouth and then closed it again.

"Told you," he said.

"I . . . what? How?"

"Remember when you learned how to suspend a ball of fire in midair?" He sat down in the dirt and faced me.

"Of course," I said. "It was only the second or third year we'd known each other. That's a child's trick."

"It's the same principle," he said, "but I'm holding the fire away from the branches, so that they can't catch the flame. The fire is all around the branches, almost intermingling with them. But it can't touch them. And they don't burn."

"I want to learn." I stood up. "Teach it to me."

"Easy there," he said. "This one took me four months of practice to master."

"I can do it in two," I said. "I want to learn it before the camp moves on to Kuhmo."

He nodded. "Go to the maze in your mind."

I closed my eyes and drew the labyrinth to mind—white

on a black background. It was laid out before me like a map, and I was a bird soaring above it. At various points in the labyrinth were symbols that I'd associated with each piece of magecraft I'd learned.

"I can see it," I said.

"Good. Now, go to the basic elements of firecraft."

I traced my way along the labyrinth until I reached the symbol I'd given the basic elements—four tent pegs in a cluster.

"Okay," I said.

The pounding of horse hooves snapped my attention away, and the labyrinth disappeared. I looked up in time to see a wagon carrying six quellers hurtle down the path, headed east. The direction of the fire. My sister's new husband rode among the quellers.

I shrank back into the trees, my heart pounding. Had they seen us? Would Darick tell Mama—or worse, the council—that I was in the forest with a boy from outside the clan?

But the quellers continued down the path without acknowledging us.

When they disappeared from view, I sank down to squat in the mud, my heart hammering. "That was close."

Nolan's face was pale. "Way too close."

My hands tingled from the fear that had replaced the blood in my veins. I needed a steady mind for magecraft. Or a steadier one, anyway. Fear made the fire unstable. Unsafe.

And we couldn't risk an accident.

Nolan put a hand on my shoulder. "Are you alright?"

I turned to face him. "Aye. Are you?"

He exhaled a long, deep breath and then muttered, "I think I will be in a minute. Gotta get my heart beating again."

"Let's pick this up again tomorrow," I said. "I should probably get back soon. There's a show tonight at the festival grounds."

"I know," he said. "I'll be there, cheering you on. And the other girls too. But mostly you."

My insides felt warm and mushy, like half-baked bread dough. What was it about this boy that made me take leave of my senses?

We stood up and embraced, his body warm against mine. "I'll look for you in the crowd," I said.

He kissed the top of my head, and I turned around and wended my way back up the path.

That really *had* been too close of a call. I had to figure out a way to get Nolan and his family readmitted to the clan. If I couldn't, the day would come when I'd have to choose between Nolan and my place among the Fintan.

And that was a choice I wasn't prepared to make.

TWO

I stood over Breanna's shoulder as she applied her black eyeliner. She sat in front of her small white vanity, along the canvas wall of the round dressing tent.

"Excited for the show?" I asked. Outside, the murmur of a burgeoning crowd was just barely discernible over the riotous folk music. In the tent, four or five troupe dancers were still getting ready for the show—me included.

"Nervous," she said, setting the pot of eyeliner down and dabbing at the crease in her eyelid. "New dances always make me jittery."

I squeezed her arm. "You'll do great. You never miss a step in practice."

"It's different when you're in front of a crowd. When the festival depends on you getting it right."

"Oh, Breanna. You always do even better in shows than in practice. That's why you're the Phoenix." I wiped away a fleck of eyeliner that had smudged too far from her lash line. "There. Perfect."

My sister had a fiercer, more intense beauty than I did. It wasn't that I hated the way I looked, or even that I envied her. But she stood out in a crowd with her aquiline nose and full lips and piercing blue eyes and cheekbones that needed no rouge or shadow to look perfect. I, on the other hand, had too round a face and smaller features, which were perfectly acceptable but far from striking.

When we were younger, people had guessed we were sisters by our flaming-red hair and tall, slender builds. But now that Breanna was the Phoenix, her hair was dyed. The brilliant red was still there, but her roots were darkened to the shade of a burnt-out ember, and highlights of every color of the eternal flame—honey-yellow, amber, tiger-orange, garnet—were mixed in with her natural red.

Now, strangers didn't recognize us as sisters.

She picked up her most dramatic set of lash feathers, small black wisps that looked like the longest of eyelashes. "Help me put these on?"

"Of course." I took the tiny tube of paste and applied tiny dots of it along her lash line. Then, carefully, I pressed the lash feathers on and brushed away a trace of dried paste left over from our last performance in Parkano.

"You look beautiful," I said.

She laughed. "You always say that."

"It's always true. Is Darick coming tonight?"

She bit her lip. "Of course he is."

Her husband never missed a show. Even when we danced five times in one week. And he always brought her flowers. It made all the other dancers swoon.

Breanna had done very well for herself, indeed. A caring husband *and* the coveted role of principal dancer in the troupe. Everything I wanted for myself someday.

Especially the role of principal dancer.

If I couldn't be a mage, I wanted to be the Phoenix with every breath in my body. My ambition craved success. And dancing—dancing as the Phoenix—was the only way for a young woman to set herself apart here in the clan.

Breanna closed her eyes and leaned over the vanity so that her hair almost touched the mirror. "I'm feeling a little ill," she murmured.

I studied her with concern. Breanna was never sick. "You going to be okay?"

After a moment, she opened her eyes. "Aye. It passed. I think I'll be alright."

"I'm sure Shayla would appreciate the chance to dance for you."

She chuckled. "I'm sure she would. But we can't let her ruin the day, can we?"

Involuntarily, my eyes traced the mirrored vanities around the room until they rested on Shayla's, on the far side of the tent. She was sitting on her bench, applying makeup, her ice-blonde hair gleaming in the candlelight. We'd been good friends once.

Not anymore.

"Hey," said Breanna. "Don't let her get to you. She's just bitter and ambitious and can't stand to see anyone else happy."

I turned back to my sister. "You'll do great tonight. I should go get ready." I backed away and walked around the edge of the circular tent, toward my own vanity.

"Do you need help with your makeup?" Breanna called.

"I can do it." I waved her off. "You like to meditate before you dance, and I'm cutting it close on time."

Nodding at the other dancers who were still getting ready, I reached my vanity—six seats down from Breanna—and sank onto the bench. I stared at my face in the mirror and reached up to touch my hair. *What a mess.* First things first. I grabbed my black-toothed comb and ran it through my hair until it gleamed as brightly as Shayla's.

Then I turned my attention to the makeup. Smoky eyes. Dramatic black eyeliner, winged at the corners. Darkened eyelashes. Rouge on my cheekbones. Shadow beneath the rouge to give my face the perfect angles. And, for the first act of the show, light brown lipstick. In the second act, I'd be wearing red, but I liked the brown better.

When I finished, I stared at myself. My show face looked so very different than my makeup-free face. I liked the difference, usually. But I hoped Nolan would be able to recognize me. Sometimes I thought the makeup made all of the dancers look the same.

I pushed up from my bench and strode to the middle of the room, where our costumes hung from long, thin poles. I found mine, measured to fit me precisely, and ducked behind a curtain to change.

I shed my loose, gauzy blouse and flowing skirt and pulled on the troupe dancer outfit—tight black pants that reflected the light and a shirt of the same material. The neckline was shaped like a vee, dipping just low enough to hint at cleavage but not enough to actually show it. A strap extended from one side of the neckline to the other, and a crosspiece ran from the middle of the strap, right at my collarbone, down to the bottom of the vee. Thinner straps, three on each side, fanned from the crosspiece to the side of the vee.

In costume, I felt mysterious and just a little bit dangerous. Bold enough, perhaps, to think that I could take my sister's place as Phoenix when she retired.

I tugged at the top so that the material was taut across my body. Then I pushed my way out from behind the curtains and returned to my vanity to run the comb through my hair one more time. Glancing around the tent, I realized that all the other dancers had left. I was the last one here. Cursing under my breath, I put on my black dance shoes, and with a final look at myself in the mirror, I strode out of the tent and toward the stage in the center of the festival.

I hated being late.

The townsfolk had already begun to arrive, admiring the brilliant torches that lit the festival in every color imaginable. Hope welled up in me as I searched the strangers, who sat at the long tables adorned with glass jars full of fireflies. No sign of Nolan. I passed the central bonfire, which rose twenty feet into the sky under Liam's watchful care. Liam and I slapped hands to wish each other luck.

Colleen—the most motherly woman in the whole clan—shepherded a small battalion of her grandchildren running wild. She gave me a wave and then returned her attention to the children with an indulgent smile.

Fireworks exploded in the sky, and phoenixflies flitted from torch to torch. Their fragile wings—just like a butterfly's—were alight with fire, shedding delicate sparks that winked out before they hit the ground. One of the phoenixflies nearest me struggled to stay aloft, its wings sparking and dimming as it floated nearer and nearer to the earth. Then its flame went out, and it fell.

I glanced up toward the stage. Almost there. But helping the phoenixfly would only take a moment. I knelt and plucked it from the ground, cradling it in my hand. When a phoenixfly's wings were extinguished, it couldn't fly until it was relit. Perhaps this one would find another phoenixfly to relight it, but I hated to abandon it to be crushed by a careless passerby.

With quick, sure steps, I marched to the nearest torch, which flamed with brilliant purple fire. My breath caught in my lungs as I held the phoenixfly out to the torch so that its wings could catch the blaze. The flame shot up higher. I pulled my hands back just as the phoenixfly's wings flared to life in shades of amethyst. It took flight, soaring upward in a circle above me and fluttering away toward the great central bonfire.

I really *was* late now. I broke into a run toward the stage and took the stairs two at a time as I whisked myself up onto the platform and back behind the curtain.

I tried to slip into the crowd of troupe dancers before Deirdre saw me, but the gray-haired woman caught my eye and cast me a scowl from where she stood beside the torch. I winced. I'd cut it close. I was the last one here. Not a good look if I hoped to be the next Phoenix.

When I turned away from Deirdre, I almost ran straight into Shayla.

She smirked at me. "Ready, cousin?" she asked in a sticky-sweet voice.

Ire bubbled in my chest. I loathed her.

I flashed her a brilliant smile. "I have a good feeling about tonight."

"Oh, me too. Be careful out there." She inclined her head, a malicious glint in her eye. "It'd be a pity if anyone tripped in the routine."

I narrowed my eyes at her. Was she . . . openly threatening me? Nay, I decided. Just trying to throw me off so I'd fail onstage, in front of Deirdre and the council and all the festivalgoers. But I didn't have a pithy comeback ready, so I turned away, fuming.

The musicians outside struck up a new song—a staccato piece fit for a parade. That was our cue. Our performance would begin with the next song.

"Places, everyone!" called Deirdre.

I looked around for Breanna and found her at once. Nodding toward Deirdre, I rolled my eyes, and Breanna clapped a hand over her mouth to stifle a laugh.

Deirdre caught the look, crossed her arms, and glared at each of us in turn.

I affected an innocent countenance and darted to the right to grab the wand I'd use in the first dance. It had a slim, black stem with a thick wick on each end. I dipped the two ends in the torch, setting the wicks on fire, and strode toward the curtain to take my place in the line of dancers.

A *boom* rent the air, the last firework to illuminate the sky until after our performance ended.

I closed my eyes and counted along with the beat of the music. *One, two, three, four, five, six, seven, eight.*

THREE

I brought my wand up and held it parallel to my body, striking the opening pose.

Five, six, seven, eight.

The curtain opened, and the crowd cheered. But I didn't pay them any attention. The torchlight on the stage burned so bright that I couldn't see the audience, and that helped me pretend they weren't there.

Except . . . I swallowed. Except that Nolan said he'd be here watching me.

Would he recognize me amid a dozen other dancers?

A single violin pierced the air, its voice slow and mournful. My sister stepped forward with graceful, flowing movements, a blazing fan in each hand. She swayed to the music, slowly at first, extending her arms high, pointing her toes, twirling the fans first one way and then the other. The tempo of the music grew faster, and the drums joined in. Breanna's dancing picked up speed along with the violin until the intricate choreography was lost in the movement of fire.

We fanned out around her, spiraling our wands around our heads as we whirled in circles. It was dizzying and exhilarating, and I hoped Nolan liked it. He'd seen the fire dancers before, of course. He'd even seen me dance.

But he'd never seen me perform with the troupe in the great fire festival of the Fintan.

Breanna disappeared from the stage for a moment, reappearing from behind the curtain with a fiery sword.

Sparks exploded around us, and the crowd cheered.

I dashed behind the curtain with the other dancers again, leaving Breanna alone to dance a solo while we handed our wands off to two mages, who gave us flaming swords in return.

When the next song began, it was up-tempo and in minor key. We leaped into jetés, one by one, mimicking attacks on Breanna with our fiery swords. Every time her sword met one of ours, sparks flew up and over the stage, lighting us in a shower of embers.

Song by song, the show progressed, telling the story of an ancient warrior who defied all odds to protect the people she loved.

It was a beautiful story. I wanted to be like that warrior. But most of all, as I watched Breanna's final solo through the crack in the curtain, I wanted to be just like my sister.

When the dance ended, we floated out onto the stage one by one and curtsied to the cheering crowd. I came up out of my curtsy and searched the crowd for Nolan, but the lights onstage were still too bright. *He'll find me later.* I walked offstage and down the stairs as the next dancer sashayed forward.

My feet hit the grass, and I caught sight of Liam and two of his friends, Killian and Bard. I didn't know why he was friends with them. I loathed them both. Maybe his head *was* addled.

Liam grinned as I ran up to them. "Great show, Kyla!"

"Are you waiting for Aislinn?" I asked with a sly smile.

He shrugged, but his eyes brightened.

"Shouldn't you be tending the central bonfire?" I raised my eyebrows. "It's too big to be left alone."

"Just wanted to see her dance," he grouched. "And say hello after. I'll go back in a minute."

"Liam's in looooove!" crowed Killian.

"Shut up," muttered Liam.

"Maybe he just came to see the best part of the show." I flashed a smile at them, daring them to contradict me.

Bard snorted. "The ornamental part of the show. Dancers are pretty and all, but we all know that the magic is the real attraction."

Liam shoved Bard. "Stop that. The dancers are a huge draw. People come from miles around to see them."

"And the dancers would be nothing without the power of the mages to make the magic and ensure the fire is safe," Bard said.

"You're just bitter about Ciara," said Liam.

Killian quirked his mouth. "You're very pretty, Kyla. You know that?"

Bard made an obnoxious kissing noise. "Is Killian in love too?"

Killian swatted his arm.

I rolled my eyes and turned to storm away, but I caught a glimpse of Nolan on the outskirts of the crowd. Thoughts of Bard and Killian and their demeaning words faded away.

"Excuse me." I pushed through the mass of bodies until I came face-to-face with him. Phoenixflies fluttered in my stomach.

"You were perfect," Nolan said.

My heart beat faster. "You saw it?"

"Every moment."

I tucked my hair behind my ear. "Could you tell who I was?"

"Of course I recognized you," he said. "You were the best dancer there."

I laughed and tugged his arm to lead him away from the stage. "Now I know you're lying. Breanna's our best dancer, and Shayla might be better than me."

"I didn't notice that," he said. "I just noticed you."

My cheeks were surely bright red. I took his hand. "Come on," I said. "Let's look at everything."

It was always a risk, walking around the festival with Nolan, but with all the Fintan focused on making the festival grand, no one had ever noticed me walking with an outsider. Or if they noticed, they didn't say anything. We'd done it on many occasions since we'd first met as children at this very festival.

But I still kept an eye out for my mama. I didn't want to explain Nolan to her yet—not until I'd figured out how to get his family readmitted to the clan.

Mama worried all the time.

Papa knew that Nolan and I were very good friends—I didn't keep much from Papa. But he didn't know about my dream to bring Nolan's family back in. Some hopes were too fragile to speak aloud.

Nolan and I cut through the crowd to the edge of the festival, past the smell of roasting meat, past the booths selling trinkets and potions made from ash, and past a storyweaver enrapturing the crowd with the help of fiery strands that flowed from his fingers. Someday, I vowed, I would practice that level of magecraft.

A vision unfurled in my mind, of Nolan and I taking our mage tests together, of entertaining the festival attendees with magecraft side by side. Then I rolled my eyes at my own thoughts. The council would never let me do magecraft in the festival—but they couldn't stop me from learning in secret. And I wouldn't stop. I was too drawn to the magic. The elemental fire serenaded me, begging me to plumb its depths.

When we reached a quiet spot, far from most of the festivalgoers, we sat together at one of the long tables, right next to a glass jar full of fireflies. The insects faded in and out, glowing one moment and invisible the next in the dark.

Ten yards away, a mage suspended a ball of flame in the air to the delight of a thronging crowd of children. He moved the position of his hands, and the ball elongated and took shape, becoming a fiery dragonbeast.

The Fintan told stories about two kinds of dragons. The

first, the dragonbeasts, which had the cunning of a person and the personality of a cat, were great lizards that flew and breathed fire. They hadn't been seen in a thousand years, some stories said. The elders said there had never been any such beast. But I didn't believe them.

The second kind of dragon were warriors, who wielded the fire with incredible power, bonded to it in a truer, deeper way than our most talented mages could ever hope to be. The dragon-warriors had vanished from the earth around the same time the dragonbeasts did. *If* the stories were to be believed.

I chuckled. No point mourning something I'd never see.

The children squealed, and I took Nolan's hand.

"I brought you something," he said, reaching into his pocket. He pulled out a smooth, shiny stone, like polished coal, and set it on the table in front of me.

I tilted my head in question.

"Light it." He traced his hand across its smooth surface. "Not right here. Not now. That would make a scene. Sometime when you have some privacy."

"Thank you." I gazed down at it. "It's beautiful."

He grinned. "You haven't even seen what it does yet."

I pocketed the coal and gazed out at the festival. "What's your favorite part of all this?" I asked.

"The food."

I rolled my eyes. "Be serious."

"I thought that should be obvious. Seeing you dance."

"Besides that," I said. "You'd come to the festival even if you didn't know me, wouldn't you?"

"Of course."

"Why?"

He ran a hand through his sandy hair. "It feels like home, I guess. I mean, don't get me wrong, my papa's always made a good life for us. Home is with him and my sister and my brothers, as well as the people my papa takes under his wing,

There's usually a few of those at any one time. But it'd be nice to have a community, you know? Something like this where we're all working together for a greater purpose. I mean, I guess my papa . . ." He fell silent.

I elbowed him. "What?"

He shook his head. "Nothing. Sorry. Just thinking. I . . . I guess I just love seeing all the beauty. Everything that the Fintan have built. Even though I wasn't raised here, it's where I come from. I want to belong here."

"I want that for you too."

He put his arm around me, and I leaned my head against his shoulder. "I know you do, Kyla. It just can't be. The council won't allow it. I know that. Deep down, I think you do too."

In the distance, the first of the sky lanterns rose up from the earth to kiss the sky. Though Fintan fire blazed in every color imaginable, we used only golden-white, blue, and purple flame in the lanterns.

It always took my breath away.

More lanterns rose into the air, the thin paper globes held aloft by the heat of the flame. They glimmered as if a thousand stars had come down to greet us and were now returning to the heavens.

"*This* is my favorite part," Nolan whispered. "Besides seeing you dance."

"Mine too." We sat there, in the silence of that perfect moment, for long time. I thanked the eternal flame that such bliss existed in the world.

When the lanterns burned through their fuel and fell dark, sinking from the sky in soft, silent waves, I focused my gaze on the glassed-in fireflies. "You know I'm not an optimist by nature, Nolan. It's not that I have blind faith that everything will work out. It's just . . ."

That I won't give up until it's done.

"That what?" he asked.

"That . . . I'm determined to see it through. And you know I don't give up on anything I put my mind to."

"Kyla, don't—"

"Kyla Brannan, what are you doing?" screeched a voice behind me.

I tensed. *Mama.*

Blazes.

FOUR

Nolan shrugged away from me and whirled around to face Mama. I stayed stock-still, staring at the fireflies, my knuckles white, my fingers clutching the edge of the rough wooden table.

"Hi," he stuttered. "You must be Mrs. Brannon. Honored to meet you, ma'am."

The distant sounds of revelry and music and crackling flame could not mask the ice in her voice. "And you are?"

"Nolan, ma'am."

Though my eyes were still fixed on the jar of captive fireflies, I heard her take a step closer, her sandals crunching in the gravel. Then her voice went up an octave. "Are you . . . Dallan Malone's son?"

"Aye, ma'am."

At this, I spun around, my taut nerves snapping like the string of a violin. "Nolan's a friend, Mama. He came to see the festiv—"

"Home. Right now." She pointed in the direction of the encampment.

"But, Mama, I—"

"Was I unclear?" she snapped. In the light, her hair—auburn red but streaked with silver—seemed to wreathe her head like a crown. She gave me an imperious look, and I knew better than to argue. Not when she was in this mood. Best to continue the conversation at home, where Papa stood a chance at calming her.

Nothing *I* could say would satisfy her.

I stood up and whispered to Nolan, "Sorry. See you soon."

Then I marched away toward my family's tent, anger hot in my chest, leaving Nolan to his unenviable interrogation.

My own would come soon enough.

I sat in the grass outside our white canvas tent, gazing up at the stars. My eyes traced the constellations—the pegasus, the phoenixbird, the dragonbeast, the dog.

I'd always loved looking at the stars. It was like they were tiny pinpricks of fire in the sky. Fire, untamed yet still safe. And that soothed me.

Reaching into my pocket, I traced the piece of coal with my fingers. A sliver of the heaviness in my chest dissipated. Maybe tomorrow I'd go down to the river, where no Fintan eyes would find me, and inspect the stone more closely—see what it did, why Nolan had been so excited to give it to me.

A deep, gruff sound from inside the tent lifted my spirits. Papa had come home first. He'd be a buffer between Mama and me.

I heard a rustle of canvas, and I stood, brushing the dirt off my pants. I hadn't even gone back to the dressing tent to replace my costume and change into my skirt and blouse. Deirdre would give me her infamous peeved side-eye when I brought the costume back the next day, but I didn't care.

I was more afraid of Mama's wrath than Deirdre's.

Pushing through the flap, I called, "Papa?"

Our tent was warm and comfortable. The coals of a small fire burned in a portable cauldron in the center, the fumes venting up through a pipe that also served as the centermost tent post.

A table with thin legs and a few chairs—all collapsible so

that they were easy to fold up and pack whenever the camp moved location—stood off to one side.

Papa was nowhere in sight, but I heard him humming in the partitioned-off room where he and Mama slept.

On the other side of the tent, another partition led to the room I'd shared with Breanna for so many years, until she married and moved out. The space was lonelier now.

"Papa?" I called again.

The humming ceased, and the canvas rustled again. Papa ducked through the flap and strode out into the main room. "You did wonderfully tonight," he said, beaming. He walked up to give me a hug, his arms spread wide, but pulled back at the last moment. "What is it?"

I grimaced. "Nolan was at the show."

He nodded, his eyes alight with amusement. "Was he, now?"

"He and I sat and talked afterward, near the edge of the festival. Mama saw us."

He wrinkled his brow. "So?"

"She wasn't happy. She's still giving Nolan a talking-to, I think."

He tilted his head and gestured to the table. "Come, sit down."

I followed him, and we each sank into chairs opposite each other at the wooden table.

"She was angry because she saw you talking with some-one from the outside?" Confusion wrinkled his weathered features.

"Um . . ." I threaded my fingers together and clenched my hands until the knuckles paled. With a desperate hope that Papa wouldn't be angry, I plunged ahead. "I was leaning against his shoulder. I think she thought he and I were . . . having a romantic moment."

His eyes softened, and a smile seemed to tug at the corners of his lips. "Were you?"

"It wasn't like that!" I said. Then I sighed. "I mean, I care about him. I . . . do think of him in that way. I think we both do. But we've never outright said it. Just hinted at it." Looking down at my lap, I blushed. "Sometimes hinting at it a lot. But at the festival, we were just talking about everything we were seeing and . . ."

"And?" His gentle voice urged me to continue, reassuring me that I would be met with nothing but kindness and understanding.

I buried my face in my hands. "That I want to find a way to help Nolan's family join the clan."

He pushed himself up from the creaky table, his footfalls heavy as he walked around the edge to join me. Amusement laced his voice as he sank into the chair next to me and rubbed my back. "You know I can't hear you when you talk into your hands like that."

I kept my fingers over my eyes but shifted my palms so I could speak audibly. "I want to help Nolan's family join the clan. Be Fintan again."

He sighed, and I heard the regret in his voice. "Oh, Kyla. It's not possible."

I sat upright and turned toward him. His eyes were serious, and I pressed my trembling lips together. I wouldn't take *no* for an answer—I couldn't. "You don't know that. I'll figure out a way." Despite my turbulent emotions, my words were clear and strong.

He tilted my chin up. "If your heart is set on this boy, I won't stand in your way. He's treated you well since you were children, and his papa's an honorable man. Dallan Malone would have raised his children well. But if you choose Nolan, you must fully realize what you're giving up. Your position in the troupe. Your life here in the community. Your relationship with our fire."

The coals in the cauldron grew redder and brighter, as if they sensed Papa's strong emotions.

"You can have a good life here," he said, seeming to choose his words carefully. "You can have a good life with Nolan, outside of the clan, apart from the Fintan way of life. But you can't have both."

I leaned forward and buried my face in his shoulder. "I don't want to leave," I said.

He pulled me into an embrace, and I relaxed in his warm, comforting presence. "I want what's best for you. What will make you happy. I just want to make sure you fully understand your decision—whatever choice you make."

The *thwack* of fabric being thrust aside told me that Mama had come into the tent. "Don't *think* we are done with this conversation, young lady!" Mama called.

"Fiona," Papa cautioned in his even, steady way. "Don't be too hard on her."

"Too . . . hard on her?" Mama sputtered. "She was consorting with Dallan Malone's son at the festival! In front of everyone! What will I—"

Papa held up a hand. "Dallan Malone is a good man. There's no cause to think badly of his son."

I looked up but couldn't meet Mama's eyes. Not yet.

"He's a defector," Mama spat. "What am I supposed to tell the parents of our young men? That Kyla's running around with an outsider? I'm tasked with finding her a steady young man for betrothal, and—"

"Mama!" My spine stiffened as straight as a rod. This time, I searched out her gaze and held it. "Nolan and I haven't even said anything about a romance. Not really."

She crossed her arms. "I saw the way you looked at each other. I'm not an idiot. I was sixteen once, too, you know."

My mind raced. "Aye. I care about him. But I'm barely sixteen. There won't be a betrothal to anyone for at least a year. And I might want to wait even longer. I don't want to rush to get married and have children. You know I want to be the next Phoenix."

She sniffed. "You can be the Phoenix if you're married."

"Not if I'm pregnant," I shot back.

She was at my side in three long strides. "You might be pregnant?" she hissed.

I stood up, rage coursing through my veins like fire. How like Mama to listen to an individual word but not to what I'd actually said. "Nay. It's not like that. Point is I don't want to get betrothed on my seventeenth birthday and married on my eighteenth. Because I don't *want* to be pregnant any time soon. I want to *do* things first. Become somebody."

Mama's eyes flashed. "Do you think I'm *nobody* because I had you and your sister?"

"Fiona," said Papa, a warning note in his voice.

I exhaled a hot breath of frustration and fought to keep my voice even. "I'm saying that marriage and family will close off some of my options because the council thinks that women need to spend all their time focused on their husband, their babies, and their tent. And that's not what I want right now."

She shook her head. "You'll think differently when you have your own children. Your whole world will change."

I slammed my hand on the table. "Everyone always says that. Stop. I don't *want* my whole world to change. Not yet. So stop griping at me for being friends with Nolan. Aye, I like him. But I'm not going to run off and marry him. Blazes, Mama. We've never even kissed."

Her eyes narrowed. "What does *you've never even kissed* mean? How long have you been running around with this boy?"

"Since we were seven, Mama. I've been friends with Nolan almost my whole life."

"Fiona," said Papa again.

She whirled on him. "You *knew*? And didn't put a stop to it?"

"He's always been good to her. Respectful." He stopped

and placed his hands gently on Mama's shoulders, and his voice grew quieter so that I had to strain to hear him. "Fiona, you know Kyla is different. Even more so than Breanna. She's not going to be content with the options available for her here, among our people. We're going to have to let her go someday, or she'll be miserable."

A chill ran down my spine.

Papa had never said anything like that to me. He'd always made it clear that I was free to stay or free to leave, that I was his daughter no matter my choice. That he wanted me to be happy. But he'd never said he thought I'd choose to leave.

My heart beat faster, and I withdrew, murmuring an apology to them both. I pushed out through the tent flap, leaving Mama's harsh, whispered reply behind.

Leave the clan? It made my stomach hurt just thinking about it. Because I didn't want to leave. I loved my family. I loved the Fintan. I loved the festival.

With a deep sigh, I plopped back down in the grass, eased myself onto my back, and stared up at the stars again.

I just wanted to *achieve* something. Something that wouldn't be dismissed as *ornamental*. Something everyone took seriously. I wanted to be successful in my own right, and not find my success in being a prop for my papa, my husband, my sons.

The drive to *be* something was so strong that sometimes it felt like it was eating me up from the inside.

But the most I could hope for was to dance as the Phoenix for a few short years before I married and began raising children.

It wasn't that I thought there was anything wrong with being like Mama. She lived for her husband and her daughters. She found her life here, in our tent. She was happy that way.

But I wasn't like her. And it wasn't fair that my options were so circumscribed. If I were a boy, I'd be in mage training.

Performing magic at the festival. Eventually, I'd work repairing the sets, teaching the children, or quelling out-of-control fires. Maybe even take a seat on the council. But as a girl, I could hope to dance. And then quit to devote all my time to raising a family. I supposed I could aspire to teach dancing, like Deirdre. But I suspected *she'd* cling to her position until the day she died.

I dug my fingers into the dirt. I just wanted *choices*.

"Kyla?" It was Breanna's voice.

I turned to see my sister coming from the direction of her tent. She wore a long, flowing dress that brushed the grass as she walked. I waved at her but didn't try to hide the emotion brimming in my eyes.

She sat down beside me. "You get in a fight with Mama?"

I sighed and wiped my tears with the backs of my hands. "It was about Nolan. She caught us talking at the festival."

Breanna chuckled and took my hand. "I always said you were taking an awful risk being with him there."

A Fintan family walked past us—a husband and wife and their four clamoring children—and Breanna and I hushed our voices to whispers.

"Papa told Mama that someday I was going to leave the clan," I murmured.

Breanna squeezed my fingers. "It wouldn't surprise me. And if you go, you'll go with my blessing."

"But I don't want to leave!" I snapped. "I just want to make something of myself. I want to be the Phoenix. I want to be a . . . mage. Blazes, why can't women be mages? It doesn't make any sense."

"You should know better than to voice that desire aloud."

I shook my head. She and I would never agree on that point.

Breanna shifted. "About that."

Something in her tone made my throat run dry.

"What?" I tilted my head.

"Well, about being the Phoenix, that is. There's something I've suspected for a month or so," she said, "but I'm quite sure after today. I wanted to come and tell you and Mama and Papa. I'm not going to be the Phoenix for much longer."

The peal of a bell sounded in my head. Her paleness. Her nausea. She'd been married six months. Something in me already knew the truth, but I asked anyway. "Why?"

She gave me a weak smile. "I'm pregnant."

FIVE

I sucked in a gasp of the cool night air. "Pregnant? That's wonderful!" Then I stopped, searching her face. "Are you happy?"

She clasped the back of her neck and leaned up against my shoulder. "Aye. I . . . I think so. I'm happy about the baby. Not about . . . everything."

I wrapped my arms around her, feeling the tension in her shoulders. "You don't want to give up dancing."

She shook her head and burst into tears.

"Oh, Breanna." I cradled her close and leaned over to kiss the top of her head. "I'm so sorry."

After a shuddering sob, she said between hiccups, "Don't . . . be sorry. It's . . . happy. A baby." She choked on the last word.

"Hey." I dug my toes into the grass to try to push down my own surge of emotion. "You have months and months to be happy about it. It's okay to feel unsure right now."

She sat up, the sobs still shaking her shoulders, and wiped her eyes. Her dramatic dance makeup smeared across her face like she was a raccoon bandit. Mine was probably just as mussed.

"How far along are you?" I rubbed her back.

"A couple months. I think."

"Does Darick know yet?"

She nodded, and this time her voice quavered but didn't break. "I couldn't cry in front of him. He was so happy. I've never seen him so happy."

I squeezed her hand, and we lay down side by side in the grass, staring up at the night sky. At the constellations. Just like we used to as children.

After a little while, I said, "I know he was equally happy on your wedding day."

She sniffled, and a bitter laugh escaped her throat. "I want to be a mama. I want to have children. Build a life and a family with Darick. But . . . there's just so much I'm giving up. And I don't know if I'm ready for that yet. But it doesn't matter, because it's here." Then a long pause. "Guess you'll get to audition for Phoenix sooner rather than later."

The idea took hold of me, tingling all the way to my fingers and toes, but I didn't let on. Not when her loss was so fresh. There would be a time to throw myself into preparation for the audition. But not tonight.

"You can dance for at least another month," I said. "Maybe two."

She sat up and brushed the dirt off her dress. Then she stared down at me. "Two. I'm determined to dance two more months. Which means we have just one month to get you ready for the audition. You're *going* to be the next Phoenix."

I pulled myself into a seated position. "I hope so," I said. "But you know that Shayla is the favorite. She's already your understudy."

She shook her head, and in the light of the stars and the torches and the fluttering phoenixflies, her face took on a deadly serious cast. "I don't care that Shayla's papa is the thane. Or that she's the understudy. I know Deirdre defers to Shayla sometimes because of her family connections, but deep down, Deirdre wants to run the most spectacular show in the land. She wants everyone to talk about her dancers. She's exacting. And I think she'll select the best dancer for the role."

That didn't comfort me. Shayla and I had such different

strengths. Who knew whom Deirdre would like more? And even if Deirdre liked *me* more, surely the council would prefer the thane's daughter.

She stood up. "Let's go inside. I want to tell Mama and Papa."

"Deirdre doesn't love me," I mumbled through gritted teeth as I stood.

"Well," said Breanna—and now there were no traces of tears in her voice, though her eyes were still puffy—"we have a month to change her mind."

"Control!" called Deirdre as we leaped through the air, practicing our jetés. "Don't lose your form. Pointed toes!"

The practice tent was getting hot and humid. Even the violinist in the corner had a trickle of sweat running down his face. I bit back the stream of retorts that rose to the edge of my tongue. Baiting Deirdre was never a good idea, and it certainly wouldn't be smart now that I was going to audition for Phoenix in a month.

Breanna had seemed more content by the time she left Mama and Papa's tent to return to Darick last night. As though she could accept losing her place as Phoenix if I could step into her dance shoes.

And I was happy because Mama had forgotten all about Nolan in her rapture over Breanna's pregnancy.

"Kyla, focus!" yelled Deirdre.

I snapped back to attention and corrected my hand placement. I'd been gripping the fan too hard.

To my right, Breanna sashayed into the tent, her face lighting up as she passed by a brilliant yellow torch. She looked as serene and at peace as I'd ever seen her, and relief rose up in my throat. I wanted this role. So badly. But not at the cost of Breanna losing it.

She strode over to Deirdre and began speaking to her in a low voice.

Out of the corner of my eye, I kept an eye on Deirdre's face and saw her nod grimly as Breanna delivered the news. It wasn't a shock, but Deirdre was surely disappointed. Breanna was an exquisite dancer.

After a minute of conversation, Breanna stepped forward. "At ease, everyone," she called. "I have an announcement."

I stopped moving and turned toward Breanna. Biting my lip, I stood straight and tall. Then I smiled at her. The moment was here.

Everything was about to change. Forever.

The movement around me stilled, and I wondered how many of the girls had already guessed Breanna's announcement. The anticipation seemed to crackle in the stuffy air.

"Wonderful news," said Breanna warmly. If she was feeling doubt this morning, she hid it well. "I'm with child and will be retiring from the troupe in two months."

The girls burst out into cheers, and my voice was the loudest of all of them.

Aislinn grabbed my arm, her eyes shining. "Baby!" she squealed.

I glanced behind me, and my eyes connected with Shayla's for the barest fraction of a moment. Her face was alight. No doubt she was already congratulating herself on her new role as principal dancer.

Not if I had anything to say about it.

When the clapping ceased, Breanna clasped her hands in front of her and bounced up and down on her toes for four beats. "I'll miss you all very much, and I expect each and every one of you to come visit me after I'm no longer here at practice with you every day. Now, Deirdre and I want this to be as seamless a transition as possible. We will hold auditions for Phoenix one month from today, which gives you all time to practice for the audition and time for the incoming Phoenix to train with me for a month before she steps into the role in shows. The audition will be the solo from Scarlet Moon."

I nodded. I wasn't surprised by the choice. We'd performed Scarlet Moon on our most recent tour through Parkano and Juankoski. Everyone was familiar with the music, and it was one of the most difficult pieces Breanna had danced as Phoenix.

It was also my favorite piece, and Breanna had already taught me some of the steps to her solo.

I hid my smile behind a fake yawn. Leave it to Breanna to figure out a way to help me dance my best.

I'd need all the help I could get to defeat Shayla.

SIX

"Nolan?" I called as I strolled down to our favorite spot by the river late that afternoon. When Mama had lit into us at the festival, we hadn't set up a time to meet. But I hoped I'd find him here.

In my fingers, I clutched a note I'd written for him. If he wasn't here, I'd leave it in the knot in the gnarled oak. We'd passed messages there before.

The river burbled happily, rushing through its sloping curves and over the thousands of speckled pebbles beneath the current. Somewhere high above me, a dove cooed. I breathed in, letting the fresh, wild smell of the evergreen forest soothe my overwhelmed heart.

"Nolan?" I called again.

The leaves rustled, and Nolan stepped out of the glade, his blond hair gleaming in the sunlight. "Hey."

The phoenixflies in my stomach did a synchronized pirouette. I tucked the note in my pocket—I had no need of it—left the path, and rushed toward him, crunching through the underbrush. When I reached him, I threw my arms around his middle and hugged him tightly.

"You okay?" he asked. "Did your mama calm down?"

I gave a deep sigh that wracked my whole body. "Let's climb the oak."

"That bad, huh?"

I strode over to the base of the tree and reached for the lowermost bough. I wrapped my hands around it, leaped, and swung myself up onto the branch. "Come on."

Nolan followed me as I scrambled from branch to branch, my muscles straining as I climbed. We reached our favorite boughs—mine just slightly higher than his—three-quarters of the way to the top of the oak, and nestled into the tree's comfortable crooks. When we were children, we'd climbed even higher, but now the highest limbs didn't support our weight.

"Mama's alright," I said as I ran my fingers along the rough bark. "She just worries about me. But Breanna's pregnant, so now Mama's going to spend the next few months in raptures and focused on nothing but Breanna."

"How does that make you feel?" asked Nolan, reaching into the leaves and plucking a couple berries off a snaking vine. He tossed one up to me and popped the other into his mouth.

"Oh, I'm happy Mama's attention is going to be elsewhere," I said, tracing the berry's smooth skin. "I'm worried about Breanna, though."

"She's not happy?"

I tilted my head. "Nay. She's . . . happy. She's just worried that it's going to make her life . . . smaller, I guess. It ends her career as the Phoenix." I glanced down to see his reaction and bit into the berry. The tart flavor flooded my senses.

He shook his head. "I can't imagine. She's worked so hard for it."

"You have no idea."

He swallowed the last traces of his berry and wedged himself into a vee in the branch so he could lie down. "So, you and Shayla going to solve the Phoenix question with a knife fight?"

I chuckled, and anticipation tingled in my feet. Or maybe they'd just fallen asleep because I'd tucked them underneath myself. "Something like that. Auditions are in a month. Breanna's going to help me prepare."

He whistled. "I wouldn't want to be going up against you."

I pulled a piece of bark off the branch and tossed it down at him. "That's because you're a terrible dancer."

"Not my fault! I can't even clap to the beat of a song," he retorted. "I was born with no rhythm."

A squirrel dropped down from above and skittered over my shoulder and down my legs, bolting for the tree trunk. When it reached the solid center of the oak, it turned around and chattered at me, as if to scold me for trespassing on its territory.

I shrugged. "Sorry."

The squirrel didn't seem entirely mollified, but it turned around and scampered back up another limb of the tree toward the canopy.

Nolan tracked it with his eyes. "It kind of reminds me of Shayla."

"Nay," I said. "It has much better manners."

The squirrel stopped on a higher branch, far out of reach, and disappeared into a hole in the trunk. Moments later, it reappeared with a tiny acorn between its paws and chucked it at me. The acorn bounced off my head. *Ouch!* I scowled up at the impudent creature.

Nolan grinned. "Still better manners than Shayla?"

I snorted. "Any fire magic you can show me up here?"

He eyed the drying leaves. "Not a chance. Not unless you can resurrect us out of the ashes like a phoenixbird in one of the old stories."

"Phoenixbird didn't resurrect itself. It just laid a fireproof egg." I chuckled and then reached up and ran my hands through the leaves above my head. "It's just so peaceful up here. It always makes me feel like we're safe. Like no one can find us."

"If you want to practice magecraft, we can go back down to the creek bed."

I dug my fingernails into the bark and shook my head. "In a little bit. Not yet."

"Need more time in the treetops?"

I glanced down at him and dangled my hand to meet his. "Just trying to memorize this moment and hold onto it forever."

Nolan flicked a spider off his shoulder. "Well, I want to show you what that rock does."

My fingers slipped into my pocket, rubbing the coal's smooth surface again. A smile broke out across my face. "Alright, then. Let's go."

The trip down the tree took longer than coming up had—I couldn't afford to sprain an ankle. *Especially* not right before the Phoenix audition. So I carefully clambered from branch to branch, taking painstaking care to place my feet and hands correctly.

Nolan, with no such reservations, arrived at the ground well before I did. "Slowpoke!" he called.

I shot him a withering glare and continued my cautious, slow descent. When I reached the last branch, I jumped to the ground, landing in a perfect crouch.

"Impressive," he said, raising an eyebrow.

"That's what happens when you dance your whole life."

He gave a flourishing bow and almost toppled over. I burst out laughing. He righted himself with a scowl on his face, but the pretense at frustration didn't mask his amusement.

"Now, then." I pulled the rock out of my pocket. "You said light it on fire?"

He tightened his lips like he was trying to suppress a grin. Then he nodded.

Laying the rock flat in the palm of one hand, I drew to mind the labyrinth map and honed in on the element represented by a single tongue of flame. "*Lasrach*," I whispered.

Lavender fire appeared in my hand, bathing the coal. I glanced up at Nolan, my eyebrows raised.

"Just watch," he said.

My attention returned to the black rock, which was

taking on a purple hue. Then a tendril of fuchsia mist curled up out of the coal like a ribbon, shaping itself into a heart that hovered above my hand. It pulsed there, and my cheeks warmed. I looked up at Nolan, and he was biting his lip, a sheepish grin on his face.

"Do you like it?"

Did I? My insides quivered. I loved it and hated it all at the same time. I longed to be close to Nolan. He was my best friend in the world besides Breanna. So much of me wanted this future with him. But I was afraid too.

Because I loved my family and my clan.

Nolan stood there before me, hope and embarrassment warring in his face. I gave him a soft smile. "Aye. I love it," I said.

He lit up, and I closed my hand and whispered, "*Múchadh*." The fire flickered out, and the coal turned cool in my grasp. I opened my hand again to study the stone, and it sat as subdued and unassuming as always. Just a little black rock.

"It was beautiful," I murmured.

He took a step toward me and closed my palm around the coal again. "I'm glad you liked it."

My mind whirled. I cared about Nolan. So much. But I wasn't ready for this. Wasn't ready to decide whether I was going to leave the clan for him or not. And even if I did, there were so many things I wanted to do first.

"I wanted to be with you when you lit it for a reason," said Nolan. His voice cracked on the last word. "I know there's a lot we've left unsaid. And maybe we should keep it that way for a while. I wouldn't have given you the token if I'd known you were going to be training for the audition right away. I don't want to pull you away from your dream. I just wanted . . . to say that I care about you. That's all. For now."

I cleared my throat. "That sounds good."

New amusement sparkled in Nolan's eyes, and I wanted

to kick myself. *That sounds good?* He'd been so eloquent, and I sounded like a stuttering child.

"I mean . . ." I continued, not at all sure that the words I was stringing together would be any more intelligent. "I mean, thank you. For understanding. That I care about you but that . . . later."

Brilliant job, Kyla.

He winked at me. "I'm doing something right if the lovely Kyla Brannon's been rendered speechless."

I rolled my eyes. "Don't flatter yourself."

At that, he laughed aloud. "Now that that's out of the way, how about some magecraft?"

I nodded, forcing myself to listen to Nolan's instructions as I began running through the magic elements I'd already learned. But my attention was half-hearted.

More than ever, I didn't want to lose Nolan, and I didn't want to lose the clan.

And despite Papa's warning, if there was any hope of keeping both, I'd fight anything and everyone for it.

SEVEN

Nolan and I practiced magecraft until nightfall. Mama cast me a suspicious glance when I slunk back into the tent to go to bed. But she didn't say anything. Papa must have talked her down before I arrived.

When I awoke the next morning, Mama was already gone, off to the market, I supposed. Or to crow to her friends that she was going to be a grandmama. Or, if she was in a bad mood, to complain about her rebellious younger daughter.

In the dawn's light, I stretched and then got dressed and set out for the practice tent. A few men were moving about the festival grounds, checking the safety of the dance stage or cleaning ashes from the cauldrons. But for the most part, all was eerily quiet. In the early light, the festival looked abandoned. Haunted.

Not a dancer in sight. I was early, but that was the point. I wanted to be there practicing by the time Deirdre arrived. To show her how serious I was about the audition.

To set myself apart from the others—especially Shayla.

When I arrived, I ducked through the tent flap and blinked to adjust to the dim interior.

Now I was well and truly alone. Humidity and the scent of sweat still hung on the air, somehow more noticeable in the isolation. I wrinkled my nose.

The torches weren't lit yet, and the faint light of sunrise only cast a gentle glow through the fabric of the tent. I'd never seen it so dark in here. I marched over to the nearest torch and whispered an incantation in ancient Eirian, cupping my hand near the torch's wick. A ball of fire blazed to life in my hand, and I held it up to the wick, smiling as the light caught and flamed bright.

Then I shook my hand to extinguish the rest of the flame. Let Deirdre assume I'd brought in a candle to light the torch, or that Papa had come with me and lit it himself. I would privately delight in the secret that I'd used magecraft.

With a satisfied exhale, I strode over to the collection of props along the tent wall. The solo from Scarlet Moon used a long wand with a flame on each end, and two fans.

The wand was easier to work with, but I couldn't wrest my gaze from the fans. An idea started to stir in the back of my mind.

An idea that no one would approve of. Except Nolan.

I gripped the fans and, first glancing back at the tent flap to ensure I had no witnesses, lit them with a whispered word.

I held them out, testing their weight and feel in my hand. Then I ran to the center of the tent and stood a moment, counting the beats of music in my head.

This was the final move of Scarlet Moon. I started in a plie, one leg extended to the floor, my toe pointed. Then my feet shifted into a tight spin, and I held one fan above my head and the other to the side so that, as I spun, it created the illusion of a seamless circle of light.

The music in my head slowed, and I came out of the spin and grasped with all my focus onto the threads of magecraft that seemed to dance around the burning fans. As I struck a pose on pointe, I twisted my wrist and mouthed a word. A shower of a thousand sparks burst out of the fan, floating to the ground as embers all around me.

I grinned. Breanna had always sent a handful of sparks flying with that move just by twisting the fans with her wrist—they were designed to cast off a few sparks. But I'd used magecraft to perfect it. To push it beyond the bounds of dancing. If only I could use it in a show —or the audition.

But it was too dramatic. Too many sparks. The council was likely to recognize it as magic.

Too bad.

I whirled around and took position again, ready to practice the move once more.

But I stopped, panic gripping my throat.

Staring at me from the entrance to the tent, her arms crossed, stood Shayla.

"What are you doing here?" I demanded.

"Practicing," she said, her voice hard. "Same as you."

An awkward silence hung between us, and I scrambled for words. "Sounds good. I'll take this side; you can stay over there." I strode a few paces away to give her more space. My heart pounded. What had she seen?

"What did you do back there?" she asked.

I turned back to study her, keeping my face relaxed and neutral. "What do you mean?"

"How'd you make the fans spark like that? Even oh-so-perfect Breanna never pulled that off. And you're no Breanna. You've just barely started practicing."

My mind lurched for an explanation but came up blank. I shrugged, hoping my face looked sufficiently mysterious. "A dancer never reveals her secrets. Especially not to the competition."

Shayla twisted a strand of golden hair around her index finger, and I held my breath. Had she seen my whispered incantation? A nagging memory started to rise up in my chest. Something I'd almost forgotten about.

After a moment, she said, "How's Nolan doing?"

My stomach churned, and that nagging memory exploded on me like a backdraft. When we were children, when Shayla and I were still friends, I'd told her once that Nolan was teaching me magecraft. She'd never brought it up again. Especially not since we stopped speaking to each other. But with one look at her face, I knew she knew.

And I feared what she might do with that information.

I swallowed. "He's doing really well. Working as a blacksmith. Still apprenticing."

She cast a long glare in my direction and then turned her back on me and strode over to the tent wall, toward the equipment.

I made a noise of frustration in the back of my throat and then moved into position to practice the spin. I didn't dare release the shower of sparks again, not with Shayla scrutinizing my every move.

But, oh, how I wanted to.

When Deirdre appeared, she nodded at Shayla and me but gave us no other reaction. I wanted to grouch that I'd arrived before Shayla, but I knew it was childish and petulant.

After just a moment, Shayla pranced over to confer with Deirdre, and I held my breath. Was she ratting me out? Telling Deirdre that I'd used fire magic while practicing my spin?

But then Shayla launched into a pirouette, and Deirdre stepped back, studying her form. When Shayla finished and looked up expectantly at Deirdre, she was rewarded with a nod and a warm smile.

I grumbled under my breath, stalked over to the water barrel, and took a long sip from the ladle. The water soothed my parched throat but not my irritation. Leave it to Shayla to get on Deirdre's good side. Probably more effective than playing schooltent tattletale. But I couldn't suppress the tendril of fear. Shayla had tucked the observation away in her pocket, just in case she ever needed to pull it out.

One by one, the other dancers arrived, and the tent

started getting warmer. It would be a scorching day—and a long one. I wiped a bead of sweat off my forehead and threw myself into a tight turn.

Practice started precisely on time, as it always did, when the violinist struck up the first melody. We spent the first half working on our routine for tomorrow night's performance, and I assiduously avoided any eye contact with Shayla. Then Deirdre announced that we were going to practice for the Phoenix audition. My heart beat faster, and I clenched my fists.

I could do this.

Breanna flitted to the front to join Deirdre, every step elegant and serene. Sorrow broke through my excitement. My sister wasn't ready to give this up. I didn't want her to lose this role. But there was no changing her pregnancy, or what it meant for her future.

Deirdre jerked her head toward the tent flap. "Anyone who doesn't intend to audition for Phoenix can go now. The rest of you, stay. Breanna and I will start teaching you the dance."

Shayla, of course, already knew the whole dance. She was the understudy, after all. And Breanna had taught me a few sections of it on our tour through Parkano. But while the other girls might know a few steps from observing Breanna, they hadn't had any cause to learn this dance yet.

Most of the dancers left—girls who had just joined the troupe, or who were about to announce a betrothal, or who were content to be a fire dancer of the Fintan, or who didn't think they had a chance of making Phoenix and didn't want to submit themselves to the arduous training.

But seven of us stayed. I studied my competition. Ciara. Nuala. Taryn. Faline. Aislinn. Not surprising.

They were worthy dancers, all of them. Any one of us stood a chance. But one dancer stood out above the others.

Shayla.

I bit my lip as Deirdre brought Shayla to the front alongside Breanna to demonstrate the dance.

Shayla's lines were refined, delicate, perfectly graceful. Even if the judging was fair, she would be difficult to beat. I'd have to work harder than I'd ever worked in my life.

Because I needed this more than I needed air.

EIGHT

I arrived home exhausted and sore and covered in sweat, longing for an endless drink of water and a long night's sleep. It wasn't nearly nighttime, but I didn't care. I wasn't meeting Nolan today—he'd said his papa needed him to work late in the smithy—and there wasn't anyone else I wanted to see.

But I drew up short when I stalked into the tent. For there, sitting across the table from my mama, was a man I'd never seen before.

A man who looked very like . . . *Nolan*.

I froze. My mind buzzed. I couldn't comprehend the scene in front of me.

"Kyla," my mama said with a too-sweet smile. "I'm sure you've met Dallan."

I bowed my head to hide my shock. "I'm afraid I haven't," I said. "It's nice to meet you, Mr. Malone. Nolan speaks highly of you." I glanced back up, hoping I'd masked my surprise.

"I wish I could say I'm as familiar with you as you are with me," he said, but his smile was gracious. It reminded me so much of Nolan's. "Your mama sent me a message a few days ago, and I had to come for myself to meet the girl my son spends all his time with. His absences the last few days make more sense now."

My mouth opened and then closed again.

He waved his hand. "To be sure, Nolan mentioned a friend. I should have inquired more closely. I didn't realize the friend to be a lovely young woman."

"Is that a problem, sir?"

"Nay. Not a problem."

Mama lost her composure and harrumphed.

"Although," he added. "*Nolan* will certainly have to explain himself. But that's not your fault, my dear."

Mama stood up and crossed over to me in two strides. Placing her hands on my shoulders, she said, "Dallan and I agree that perhaps you and Nolan shouldn't spend so much time together."

A flash of something that looked like consternation crossed Mr. Malone's face, like he'd started to correct Mama but then thought better of it. I liked him more already.

"Well," I said, "that's something Mr. Malone can take up with Nolan. And something you and Papa can come to an agreement on."

A chuckle escaped Mr. Malone, and Mama shot him a withering glare.

"If you'll excuse me"—I slipped past Mama to the small water bucket on the corner of the table, bringing a ladleful to my lips—"I've had a long day of practice, and I'm exhausted."

I chugged another ladleful of water and then turned around and glided through the tent flap into my room. Mama didn't dismiss me, but neither did she stop me.

"Well," she huffed from the main room. "I never. I'm terribly sorry for Kyla's rudeness, Dallan. It was good to see you. It's been a long time."

Mr. Malone's reply was too low for me to make out, but I could hear him stand up. Relief flooded me.

It wasn't that I didn't want to meet Nolan's family. On the contrary. But not like this. Not with my hair plastered to my head with sweat. Not when Mama had ambushed me. Certainly not with Mama apologizing for me when I didn't respond the way she wanted me to. I sank back on my bedroll.

The tent rustled, and Papa's voice filled it

"Well, I'll be," he called in a cheery voice. "Dallan Malone, back from the dead."

I stifled a smile. Leave it to Papa to defuse a tense situation. He was used to Mama's schemes by now, and I didn't imagine he was at all surprised to find Mr. Malone at our table.

The voices faded away as the tent fabric shifted again, and I guessed that Mr. Malone and Papa had left. Maybe Mama too. I relaxed more deeply into my bedroll but shuffled the blankets aside. Too warm for blankets.

But I couldn't relax fully. Couldn't quiet my mind. I thought back to this morning, when I'd met Shayla's eyes across the tent. I'd been so immersed in the dance that I hadn't heard her come in.

And she knew my secret. She'd seen me use magecraft.

Did she think I was planning to use magecraft to beat her in the audition? It wouldn't be cheating, exactly. There was no formal rule against it. There didn't have to be, since women weren't instructed in magecraft. But she had nothing to worry about. If I used forbidden magic, I risked the council detecting it. Questioning me. If they ever found out how versed I was in magecraft, they'd demand to know where I'd learned it.

I flipped onto my side and clutched my pillow to my chest as if it could block out all the pain and doubt in my world.

I wasn't ready to tell the council about Nolan yet. Not until I'd figured out a way to convince them to give Nolan's family another chance.

They weren't likely to look kindly on a defector who'd taught magecraft to his son, nor on a young man who had taught it to a woman.

Nay, the risk was too high. The secret was too dangerous. We needed to be sure our plan would work before we acted.

But if Shayla thought I was scheming, would she sabotage me? Would she tell her papa, the thane? Or the rest of the council? Or Deirdre?

My thoughts raced. Might she try to have me disqualified from the audition? Kicked out of the troupe? Thrown out of the clan altogether? I didn't think her animosity ran that deep, but after so many years of hatred between us . . .

The thought sent a shiver through me despite the stuffy air. I squeezed my pillow more tightly.

I couldn't just *talk* about formulating a plan to get Nolan admitted to the clan. For years I'd thought about it, but always as something to do "someday." But if Shayla knew—about the magecraft, about Nolan—I was running out of time. If Shayla decided to tell her papa about my magecraft . . . I could be kicked out of the troupe. Even expelled from the clan if the council was in a bad mood. Nolan's papa might even be dragged before the council and put on trial for practicing and teaching the elemental fire outside the clan.

And if Shayla could win the Phoenix role by ruining my life, I didn't think she'd blink.

I needed to figure out how I'd plead with the council. And soon.

If I didn't, I'd lose Nolan forever.

The gravel crunched beneath my feet as I hurried down the path. It had been another long day of practice, and I'd barely taken the time for a sponge bath before racing out of the tent to find Nolan.

I hoped he'd be at our usual meeting place by the creek. That his papa wasn't keeping him home. Dallan had seemed friendly enough, but almost . . . perturbed. *Does he not want us to be friends? Will he try to stand in the way, like Mama?*

My thoughts circled in on themselves as I angled off the path and ducked into the grove.

Nolan was waiting in our usual spot, perched on the edge of a rock on the riverbank, dangling his feet into the current.

The tension in my shoulders released. I joined him on the rock, plunging my sandaled feet into the cool water. After another long day of dancing, it felt like paradise.

"You okay?" I asked, brushing my hands on the rock's mossy surface.

He shuffled to the side to make room for me and ran a hand through his sandy hair. "Did my papa come to visit you yesterday?"

"Aye. I think Mama invited him."

He splashed the water with his foot. "What'd he say?"

"Not too much." I chuckled. "I slipped away pretty quickly. Didn't know what to say. Mama sprung the whole situation on me. What'd he tell you?"

He reached out and took my hand. Warmth flooded my stomach.

"He's worried about me," he said. "But he tries not to show it."

"My papa's like that too. Mama doesn't want me to see you anymore, but Papa . . . he . . ." I blinked rapidly. "He told me he doesn't think I'll stay with the Fintan forever."

Nolan reached out and cupped my chin. "Does that surprise you?"

I shrugged away from him and gazed down at the rippling water. "I've just never pictured myself leaving before. Not really. My family is here. My whole life is here, except for you."

"Why does your papa think you'll leave?"

I lost myself in the rippling current for a moment to try to numb the pain in my chest, and then I said, "He doesn't think I'll be happy here. He thinks my ambitions are too big for the festival. At least since I'm a woman and the council doesn't give me many options."

"Do you think he's right?"

I reached down, plucked a pebble out of the mud, and tossed it into the creek. "I wish I knew. I want to be like Breanna. To dance as the Phoenix. But I want more than that. Always have. I want to be a mage."

Nolan leaned back, gazing up at the pink-and-orange tinted sky. "What if we've been thinking about this the wrong way?"

I pulled my feet out of the water and propped them on the rock to dry. "What do you mean?" I didn't think I was going to like his answer.

"I know . . . what I said before. That I didn't want to push you to make any decisions too young or too fast. And I meant it. Every word. But what if your papa's right? What if we shouldn't be thinking about ways to get my family in, but how to get you out?"

I bit down hard on my lip. Was it foolish of me to hope that life wouldn't demand sacrifices of me? To think that I was special, that somehow I could have everything I wanted? A life with Nolan? A place in the clan? The chance to practice magecraft in the open? To—someday—have babies and take care of them *and* make a name for myself as a mage?

Nay. When I thought about it like that, when I laid out the future I so desperately wanted, not even I could raise my hopes that high. That didn't mean I wasn't going to try for it. But I needed to prepare myself. To recognize that, if I failed, I'd face a difficult choice.

"I'll think about it," I said.

He heaved a long sigh. "This is the biggest decision of your life. Take all the time you need."

NINE

I flicked a pinch of flour into Breanna's hair.

"Hey!" she said, her jaw dropping in mock outrage. She ran her hand through her fiery tresses and then dipped the ladle into the bucket and flung a splash of water at me.

I shrieked and ducked away before returning to the table, laughing, pulling my sweater tighter around myself on this unseasonably cool day.

We were in Breanna's tent, baking bread. It was the troupe's day of rest, and my sore muscles told me I'd earned it.

Deirdre always worked us hard, but training to audition for Phoenix was exhausting. My admiration for Breanna had climbed to new levels this week. And I was grateful to get to spend this time with her on our day off.

I reached for the butter and whispered, *"Lasair."* A tiny flame surged to life in my hand, and I held it up to the butter to soften it.

Breanna crossed her arms, concern shadowing her eyes. "It's dangerous for you to be doing things like that in camp, you know."

I looked around the tent, my gaze resting on the bouquet of fresh wildflowers perched in a vase on the table. "Who's going to see me? Even Darick isn't here."

She shrugged, walked up alongside me, and watched as I finished softening the butter and dropped it into the mixture of flour and water and salt. She stirred the dough together, and I extinguished the flame.

"I just don't like seeing you take unnecessary risks," she said softly. "I'm like Mama in some ways, I guess."

The dough was too wet, so I reached for the bag of flour and poured a little more into the bowl. "How are you feeling about everything now?"

She sighed. "I'm happy, Kyla. I really am. My life is so very good, and I'm thankful." But tears brimmed in her eyes. "I just still haven't let go of it all."

I took a deep breath, inhaling the scent of fresh-cut flowers. Breanna's tent always smelled like flowers. Then I rested my hand on her shoulder. "That's okay. You still have a lot of days to figure it out."

She wiped at her eyes, leaving a streak of flour on her cheekbone. "I *shouldn't* be ambivalent, right? I mean, I'm pregnant. I've always wanted to have children. It's just . . . I always thought I'd be happier than this."

A pang of concern twinged in my chest. "Are you okay, Breanna?"

She laughed, but it was dull and hollow. "Aye. I will be. I just want to feel like *me* again. And trading in dancing for nappies doesn't feel like me. I'm sure I'll feel differently when the baby comes."

Hot anger burned in my core, and I took a long, slow breath. I had to contain the rage so that I didn't accidentally set something on fire with a burst of magecraft. There was no reason Breanna should have to give up dancing. For a few months, sure—right before and after the birth. But permanently?

And suddenly I couldn't reassure her that everything would be alright. Because I wasn't sure that I believed it anymore. "It's not fair that they're asking you to," I said. "You should be able to dance again after the baby is born."

She dug her hands into the dough and pounded it against the bowl. "Nay. It's not fair. I hate this. I hate all of it." The bowl came up off the table and slammed back down with the force of her momentum.

She stared at it.

Breanna never had outbursts.

"Have you talked to Darick about how you feel?" I asked.

She sniffled. "What good would that do? He can't change the laws."

"He can't." I pulled out a chair and sank onto it. "But it could let him know that you're feeling conflicted. That he should be more sensitive to all that's changing for you."

She stopped kneading and picked up a towel to set over the bowl while the dough rose. Then she took a seat on the floor next to my chair and leaned her head against my knee.

"I've thought about it," she finally said. "But I don't want to disappoint him. He's still just so happy about it. He can hardly contain it." Her voice caught. "I don't want to make him feel like I don't want this, or that there's something wrong with me, or that I won't love the baby—"

"Nay." I reached down and tilted her chin up. "You listen to me. It's okay to not be sure how you feel about all of this yet. It's really okay. And you'll be a great mama to your little one. But don't beat yourself up. It's not fair that you have to give up everything you've worked toward."

She sighed, and tears brimmed in her eyes. "It never seemed to bother Mama. She didn't even make Phoenix."

"Maybe it didn't bother Mama," I said, "but you and I have always been more like Papa. You don't have to worry about measuring up to Mama. You're different than she is. Your strengths are different. And that's fine."

"If you say so."

I snorted. "Wouldn't you rather be like Papa, anyway?"

At that, she laughed. "I suppose so." Then she exhaled a long, shuddering breath. "I just need more time, I guess."

"Well, that baby's going to be in there a while." I gestured toward her midsection. "Just . . . tell Darick. Please? He needs to know so he can be supportive. You know he will be. He adores you. More than anything."

She grabbed my wrist. "Promise me, Kyla." Her eyes sought out my face and locked onto mine. "You won't give up on your dreams. You won't let the clan's rules trap you."

I eased off the chair and sat cross-legged next to her. "I'm so sorry you feel trapped, Breanna."

But she didn't release me from her intense stare. "Promise me."

"I . . . don't know what I'm promising," I said. "I'm going to work as hard as I can to become the Phoenix. And I'm still practicing magecraft."

"Good. That," she said. "We'll make you the Phoenix, and then we'll figure out a way to make the council let you become a mage. The first female mage in Fintan history."

I held up my hand and pressed my palm against hers. "I thought you didn't approve of me practicing magecraft in camp."

She sighed. "I was wrong to say that. I get nervous for you sometimes . . . but I shouldn't. Because I don't want to be like Mama. I want you to make your own choices." Her eyes smoldered, but now it was with determination, not with anger. "And I want the council to know what the Brannan women are made of."

TEN

When I arrived at the creek that afternoon, Nolan wasn't there yet. Hopefully he'd get here soon. There was another show tonight, so I couldn't stay long. I sat on the rock and stared into the rippling water, thinking over my conversation with Breanna.

I was worried about her. For all my soothing words, what if she couldn't accept her new reality? What if she resented Darick? Resented the baby? How would she cope with the long, inescapable years?

I didn't want to watch the light go out of her eyes, to see her waste away, become a shell of her former self. I'd seen that happen to women in the clan before.

Nuala's mama had killed herself when Nuala's little brother was just two months old. She'd started withering away shortly after the birth and never recovered. Nuala had sworn since we were small that she'd never marry. My own aunt—Shayla's mama—had died giving birth to a stillborn child when we were eleven.

It wasn't always that way, of course. I thought of Mama. And of Colleen, who found her joy and purpose in nurturing her children and grandchildren—and everyone else she encountered. Of Aislinn's mama, who had been so desperate for a child that she'd made a sacred vow to the eternal flame, to worship it an hour out of every day if it granted her the child she longed for. A year later, Aislinn was born.

But I wasn't like Mama or Colleen or Aislinn's mama.

I swallowed. *Promise me you won't let the clan's rules trap you.*

Shifting to my knees, I turned and stared at the bush that Nolan had set not-quite-ablaze a few days earlier. I tilted my head. Could I do it?

The knowledge that it was foolish tugged at the back of my head. I'd only seen the element done once. But Breanna's face burned in my mind. I *wouldn't* let them trap me. I wouldn't let them take my choices from me.

I focused on the open air between the branches, going deep inside my mind and summoning the eternal flame. What word had Nolan said he used? It came to me all at once. *"Moscai."*

When I opened my eyes, a tiny ball of fire hovered amid the branches, not touching any of the twigs or leaves. I stilled my mind, willing the fire to grow and spread, leaving the boughs untouched. It thickened and flowed, weaving its way around the foliage . . .

And then the bush burst into blazing flame.

I bolted to my feet and darted toward the bush, calming my fluttering mind and reaching for the quelling magic. With one hand outstretched, I raised my other into the air and whispered, *"Brú."*

"Kyla!"

The fire winked out of the bush, leaving half its branches blackened and smoking.

I stared at the bush. I couldn't turn to look at Nolan.

"What were you thinking?" he demanded.

"That I'm not going to be trapped," I muttered.

"What . . . are you talking about?"

I huffed, even though I knew he didn't have the context to understand. Embarrassment suffused my face. "It was a conversation with Breanna. She's still sad and upset and confused. And she feels trapped. And she doesn't want me to end up feeling that way." My words came out rapid and clipped.

He looked hurt. "Do *I* make you feel trapped?"

My defensiveness melted away, and I whirled to face him.

"Nay. Not at all." I rushed to his side and grabbed his hands. "I'm sorry. I didn't mean to make you think that. I just . . . it was humiliating to be caught like that." I swallowed. "I needed to be thorny, or I was going to cry."

He relaxed a little. "Sit down." He nodded at the rock, and we perched on it, arms linked.

"What makes you feel trapped?" he asked.

It should be an easy question to answer, but my mind raced. "The Fintan's rules, I guess. The expectation that I'll dance for a little while, because that's the only way for girls to distinguish themselves, and that afterward I'll settle down and give it all up."

"So, you don't want to settle down?"

His features were neutral, and gratitude swelled in my chest. He was trying to set his feelings aside to talk me through this. This sort of thing was why I loved him so much. Then my blush intensified. *Love like a friend. Care for.* I *did* think of him romantically. But it was confusing to think that I *loved* him that way. But I knew I loved him as my best friend.

Batting my churning thoughts aside, I said, "I don't want to give it all up."

"I see." He quirked his lips. "And you were feeling angry about this years-distant future possibility."

I chuckled, but it came out almost like a yelp. "Aye. And . . . angry about what's happening now to Breanna."

"And so you . . . set the bush on fire?"

This time I released a real laugh, my shoulders relaxing. "I wasn't trying to. I swear it. I was trying to weave the fire around the branches, like you showed me the other day."

He grumbled, "You know there's a word for people who set things on fire because they're upset."

"Toddlers?"

His gaze turned more sober. "Arsonists."

He couldn't be serious. "I told you it wasn't on purpose."

He shook his head, and when I looked down at his arms, I could see goosebumps prickling on his skin. "I know it wasn't," he said. "I'm sorry. I'm not really thinking about you. There's been a lot going on in the last few months. Too many fires, like I said."

My mouth went dry. Was there an . . . arsonist in Orivesi? There hadn't been an arsonist in my lifetime. "What are you—"

He held up his hand. "I'm sorry. I shouldn't have put that on you. I'm wound too tightly about it. There was another fire yesterday—small, easily put out by the quellers. Even with the dry weather, it's too many to be a coincidence. The quellers stopped by the farm to ask us questions about it. I've had suspicions for months, now, that something wasn't right. That someone's been starting blazes. But I don't know what to do about it."

"The local people will blame the Fintan," I said. The council took arson as seriously as murder, even if no one was injured. If the Fintan gained a reputation for using their magecraft carelessly, people would lose their appetite for our show.

And our show was what kept us prosperous.

Not to mention the lives that could be lost if there really was an arsonist on the loose.

"And the Fintan will blame the *defectors*," he said bitterly. "And I don't know that they'd be wrong to do so. If there is an arsonist, it could well be someone capable of wielding the magic but who lacks the training and discipline of the Fintan fire mages."

"Which was why the quellers knocked on your door yesterday."

"Aye," he said softly. "We know most all the defectors in Orivesi."

"This day just keeps getting better and better." I buried my face in my hands.

He gave a long, troubled sigh. Then his voice grew gentler. "I'd like to make it better."

"How?" I peeked at him through my fingers.

A smile overtook his rumpled face, and he reached out and cupped my chin. "I want you to spend a day with my family next week. On my day off. If you can spare the time away from practice."

I dropped my hands and stared at him. "You want me to meet your family?" *After all this time?*

He smiled. "Aye. And Papa wants you to come visit. I should have told them about you sooner. Brought you home to spend time with them. I always wanted you to meet them, it's just . . ."

I nestled into his shoulder. "I was the same way. You were worried about what they'd say."

"I don't know why," he said. "My papa doesn't love the clan leaders, but he's never forbidden me from having Fintan friends. And if he thought you and I were thinking about . . . well, he says he's never regretted marrying my mama, even though that meant he had to leave the Fintan."

I tried to hide my smile as Nolan stumbled over his words.

"I can't wait to meet them," I said. "And I promise I won't even set any bushes on fire."

ELEVEN

"Aislinn!" I hissed, poking at the canvas tent. I knew she was in there. I could hear her snoring. She sounded like a giant boar.

"Hmmph," said a muffled voice.

I bit back a smile. "Aislinn!" I whispered again, trying to keep quiet enough that I wouldn't wake her parents. But I wasn't too worried. They slept on the far side of the tent, to drown out Aislinn's snores as best as they could.

"Kyla?" She sounded groggy.

"Let's go," I said. "Time for practice."

"The sun's not even up yet. We had a show last night. I was out late."

With Liam? I smirked. "Gotta get in some extra practice and impress Deirdre."

There was a shuffling sound, and then she muttered, "Give me a minute."

It took her five minutes, but she joined me outside the tent, her dark blonde hair tied back with a ribbon and her eyes drooping.

"Come on." I nudged her in the ribs. "We got this. We're going to smoke Shayla."

She yawned and started shuffling toward the festival grounds beside me. "If you say so. Oh. That reminds me. Last night, after you left the dressing tent, Shayla was over at your vanity. Looked like she was riffling through your stuff."

I rolled my eyes. Of course she was. It bothered me, but

I shrugged it off outwardly. But I tucked the information away, determining to go through everything carefully today to make sure she hadn't planted anything.

The festival grounds were quiet again this morning, and excitement rose in my chest. Another day of practice. Another day to pursue my dreams. I wouldn't fail. Even though everyone expected Shayla to be crowned Phoenix, I knew I stood a chance. I'd focus on my strengths.

Shayla was already practicing when we arrived, and Aislinn and I both ignored her. I started stretching on the far side of the tent, while Aislinn dragged herself to the water barrel.

When my muscles felt relaxed and limber, I picked up two fans and marched over to the lit torch to set them ablaze.

It wouldn't do for Shayla, of all people, to see me use magecraft to light the fans.

Though I'd delight in the look on her face.

Shayla and I ignored each other as we danced to Scarlet Moon, but I gave Aislinn an encouraging nod now and then. We'd been at it an hour when Ciara glided into the tent and pulled up short, looking at us.

"I see I'm not the only one with this idea," she said wryly.

But she and I smiled at each other. We'd never been close, but I liked her. I shifted a few paces backward to give her room to practice.

I'd just launched into a triple turn when Deirdre walked in. I kept my attention on a single point in the corner of the tent, trying to keep my balance, willing myself to execute the move to perfection.

When I completed my rotations and held my center, Deirdre nodded approvingly at me. I wanted to pump my fist in the air, but I settled for a triumphant smile.

"Shayla. Ciara. Aislinn. Kyla," Deirdre said, nodding at each of us. "Glad to see you here so intent on your work."

"Thank you," I murmured.

"Deirdre," Ciara called, "could you help me with the second section?"

Deirdre turned her attention to Ciara, and I set the fans down with the other props. I was done with that section. When I turned around, Shayla was beside me, handing me a two-headed wand.

"Here," she said. "Are you using this next?"

"Uh. Aye. Thanks." I took it from her, and she strode away again, her hips swaying, another two-headed wand grasped in her other hand.

I narrowed my gaze at her. Why was she playing nice all of a sudden?

But there was no point worrying about it. I could only focus as hard as I could on preparing for the audition.

The tent flap opened, and two more troupe dancers came in. It was almost time for practice to start in earnest. I ran over to the torch and lit both ends of the wand. Hopefully, there was time for me to get just a little bit more work done before Deirdre called us to order.

I threw out my hand to one side and extended my leg behind me, striking the opening arabesque. *Five, six, seven, eight.*

I launched into the first step and swung the wand up above my head, tossing it into the air and twirling halfway around before I caught it. I curved my hand back and threw it high again. Just as it reached its zenith, one of the flaming heads exploded, sending tiny pieces of the wand flying across the tent.

The rest of the wand fell to the ground with a *thud.*

I stared at it, my face flushing, my heart pounding. What had just happened? Had I somehow caused the explosion with magecraft? I searched my memory. Nay. I was sure I hadn't manipulated the fire in any way. Had—

Oh.

"Kyla!" Breanna shrieked, flying to my side. "Are you okay?"

Every eye in the tent was on me. I didn't respond. The anger pulsing through me was too intense.

Deirdre swept toward me, her skirt rustling. "Are you alright, dear?" she asked, grabbing me by the shoulders.

"Aye . . ." I said slowly, looking over her shoulder at Shayla.

She smirked back at me and gave a nonchalant shrug.

Treacherous little snake.

She'd tampered with the prop. Sabotaged me out in the open.

Shivers overcame me, and I closed my eyes and reached for Breanna's hand. The explosion was small. It *could* have been catastrophic, but really, my injuries were unlikely to have been severe, even if it had erupted in my hand.

But they might have been enough to keep me out of the audition.

Or worse.

One thing was clear. Shayla was determined to be Phoenix. And she was willing to eliminate the competition by any means necessary.

But I wouldn't let her.

My eyes snapped open again, and I stepped backward. "Aye," I said. "I'm alright."

Breanna studied me. "I've never seen a malfunction like that. Do you want to go home and rest? You've had a shock."

I shook my head fiercely. "I'm here to dance. I'm not going to let that stop me."

Deirdre's eyes narrowed. "Very well. Everyone, let's get this mess cleaned up."

I shrugged away from them and set to work gathering the nearest pieces of shrapnel.

When I looked up again, my eyes met Shayla's.

Two could play this game.

If Shayla would win at any cost, so would I.

Not that I'd hurt her. Or even sabotage her. But I did

know magecraft. And it wasn't against the rules to use it in a dance. I just had to work it in with enough subtlety that Deirdre and the council wouldn't notice.

If Shayla wanted so badly to see me lose, I'd make sure that I danced perfectly. And I'd let the flourishes of magecraft carry me to victory.

TWELVE

The days passed in an exhausting rhythm of dance practice, interspersed with brief, stolen moments with Nolan. By the time the seventh morning—and my next day off—arrived, I was beyond exhausted.

I just needed to survive two more weeks, to the audition. And then give the performance of my life.

But today, I wouldn't even think about dancing. Today, I was going to meet Nolan's family.

My stomach tingled. Nolan had talked about his family in bits and pieces over the years. I knew he had two brothers and a younger sister. His mama and baby brother had been killed in an accident when he was quite small—she'd been gone for a couple of years when we met at age seven in the crowded fire festival.

I'd told him all about Mama and Papa and Breanna and life among the Fintan. But he'd always been vague on details of his family. It had bothered me a little, but when I'd pushed it once, he'd lost his temper. Yelled that he didn't want to talk about it. Later he'd told me that he was there when his mama died. Saw her and the little one burn to death. And that those weren't memories he wanted to relive.

I couldn't imagine such pain.

I laced up my boots and pulled on a demure skirt that fell in gauzy waves to the ground. Then I selected a loose, flowing top and clasped on a silver necklace to complement the outfit. At last, I tugged a comb through my long red hair and added a touch of black mascara to darken my lashes.

Perfect.

I so wanted them to like me. Especially his sister. With a final glance in my small, handheld mirror, I pushed out of my small room and crossed the main tent, launching into the open air with a giggle.

Thank the eternal flame Mama wasn't here to question where I was spending the day. She was off with Breanna, making clothes for the baby. I felt so free.

I looked for Papa as I left, but he was nowhere to be seen. Probably in the shop, working on repairs to the festival torches. I thought about stopping in to say goodbye, but a glance at the clock tower in the center of camp warned me I'd be late if I didn't hurry.

I jogged down to the creek, to our usual meeting spot among the trees. Nolan would pick me up there, and we'd walk to his family's farm, which had been passed down to them from his mama's family. His older brother and younger sister ran the day-to-day of it, he'd said, with the help of two hired earth wizards. Nolan and his other brother and their papa had their share of farm chores but put their elemental fire to use running a smithy. But Nolan still loved the farm. Said, in a less guarded moment, that it reminded him of his mama. I couldn't wait to see it.

Nolan was waiting on the mossy rock when I arrived, and he turned around at the sound of my footsteps. His eyes lit up. "You look beautiful," he said.

I blushed. "Thank you." I drew near and batted at an out-of-place strand of hair that stuck out from his shaggy mane. "You don't look so bad yourself."

"Come on," he said. "We're all going boating on the lake first, and then we'll eat at the farm."

Boating?

Nerves fluttered in my stomach. I'd never really been in a boat before, and I wasn't entirely sure I wanted to. Give me a roaring fire any day. Or the cascading water of a creek or mountain stream. But to be out on a piece of wood in the middle of a vast lake?

I swallowed. But I didn't want to look fearful in front of Nolan's family, so I jutted my chin upward. "Let's go."

He grabbed my hand, and we followed the creek downstream for a couple of miles, my apprehension building with every step. We broke from the trees where the creek fed into a vast, blue lake, its surface as smooth as a glassy mirror. On the shore in the distance, three men and a girl stood next to two small boats.

This is it. Time to meet Nolan's family.

"Are they going to like me?" I murmured.

"Of course," he said. "My papa was very impressed with you."

"But you said he seemed unsure," I said.

Nolan's sandaled feet squelched in the mud. "I think he wasn't quite sure about me spending so much time with a Fintan fire dancer, but he told me more than once that he'd enjoyed getting to meet you. In his words, 'She seems like a fine young woman.' Don't worry."

Too late for that.

We took off, walking along the bank toward the Malones. "What should I talk to your sister about?" I asked, and I hardly recognized my strangled voice.

With a little laugh, he said, "Anything you'd like. I'm sure she'll want to hear about what it's like to be a fire dancer. She loves going to the festival."

"But I don't want her to think I just like to talk about myself. What's she interested in?"

He shrugged. "She's fourteen. She likes phoenixflies and kittens and the boy on the neighboring farm."

I pursed my lips at his condescending tone. "Well, I can't talk to her about *boys*," I snapped. "Because she's your sister, and we're . . . well, I don't know what we are."

He laughed and slung his arm around me. "Just relax. It's going to be great."

Easy for him to say.

After a few more steps, I gave a shy wave at his family.

The boys called out to us, while Nolan's papa reached into the boat for something. Nolan's sister was looking in our direction, too, and I couldn't quite read the expression on her face.

Would she like me? Was she as nervous to meet me as I was to meet her?

The gravel crunched beneath my boots as we approached. Nolan removed his arm from my shoulders and took my hand.

"Kyla," he said, "I'd like to introduce my family. You already know my papa, Dallan. These are my brothers, Aidan and Hogan, and my sister, Zaira."

I curtsied. "I'm so pleased to meet all of you." When I came up out of the curtsy, my gaze rested on his brothers for the first time, and I startled.

One of them was bearded, with a thinner nose and darker hair than Nolan's. Perhaps a couple years older. But one of them seemed to be Nolan himself standing in front of me. I looked between them. It was like seeing Nolan in a mirror.

Nolan chuckled, "Aidan's my twin. We're identical."

"Your twin?"

A flash of anger wormed its way through me. I'd known Nolan for almost ten years, and he'd never mentioned an *identical twin*?

Did I know him at all?

But I locked the thought away to consider later. I wouldn't quarrel with him in front of his family.

I smiled at Aidan and Hogan and turned to Zaira. "I'm so excited to meet you," I said. "Here, I brought you a gift." From the pouch tied around my waist, I pulled out a thin gold chain with a pendant of garnet and ruby and citrine and fire opal. A pendant of fire. I stepped forward and held it outstretched in my cupped hand.

She moved toward me, and her eyes widened as she took it. "It's beautiful," she breathed. She looked up at me, and in her eyes, I read the same shyness I felt.

I wasn't accustomed to the experience of shyness. But I so wanted to make a good impression.

"Will you help me put it on?" she asked. She turned around and tucked her dark hair to the side, and I threaded the chain around her neck and clasped it for her. She clutched the pendant in her fingers and looked down at it as she turned around and faced me.

"Thank you." She pulled me into a hug.

That was a relief.

"Hey, now," Hogan said in a voice deeper than Nolan's. "No gift for me?"

I looked up at him, my eyes wide. But he was grinning.

Nolan leaned forward and punched Hogan in the arm. "Hey, now, no teasing."

Hogan guffawed. "Shouldn't have brought her here if she can't handle teasing."

I crossed my arms. "I can handle teasing."

"Ooooh," crowed Hogan and Aidan in unison.

Hogan nodded at me. "I like you, Kyla girl."

Nolan's papa cleared his throat. "Shall we be off?"

I curtsied toward him. Even though I'd already curtsied once. "Thank you so much for having me on your family outing," I said.

He gave me a gentle smile. "We're very pleased to have you with us, my dear. Come on. Let's get in the boats. Nolan, why don't you and Kyla take Zaira in one, and your brothers and I will go in the other?"

I tried to maintain a neutral expression as I stepped toward the boat that Nolan's papa was pushing into the water.

Zaira scampered in first, and then Nolan stepped up to its side and held out his hand to help me in. I took it and stared at the boat. Nolan's papa still held it steady.

"Just step in," Nolan said.

I willed myself forward, my heart pounding. What was I so afraid of? The water was just ankle-deep here.

But I didn't want to fall in and look stupid in front of Nolan's family.

I lunged at the boat, leaping to clear the edge, and ended up face-first in the bottom, the whole vessel rocking wildly. Zaira shrieked. Water spilled over the edge and dampened my skirt. I sat up, trying to keep my face serene and dignified, but Nolan and his brothers were doubled over laughing.

"It wasn't that funny," I muttered.

"You . . . should see . . . your face," Nolan managed.

I glanced over at his papa and saw that he, too, was struggling to maintain a serious expression, so I turned around and half crawled to a board that seemed to form a seat. Smoothing my wet skirt, I sat and faced Zaira. She smiled at me, but it seemed sympathetic, not like she was making fun of me.

Stupid menfolk.

Nolan scampered into the boat behind me, two oars in tow. He tossed one to Zaira, and she caught it in midair.

"I can help paddle," I said.

Nolan waved me off. "Get used to riding first. We'll teach you how to paddle once you're comfortable on the water."

Zaira tilted her head. "Are you not in boats often?"

I shuffled a hand through my hair. "I've never been in one," I said. "Well, I guess I was in one when I was about ten. When the Fintan did a tour in Napoli. But it was much bigger than this one. I could hardly tell I was on the water at all."

The boat was gliding out onto the pristine lake now, sending ripples out in every direction. When I glanced back at the shore, Nolan's papa and brothers were climbing into their boat, the whole forest stretching out behind them like a living emerald.

"We come out here whenever the weather's nice," said Zaira. "Papa says my mama loved water, and she taught him to love it too."

I hazarded a glance behind me at Nolan and then focused back on Zaira. "What was your mama like?"

She shrugged and looked down at the bottom of the boat. "I don't really remember much about her. She had dark hair, like Hogan and me. She sang a lot. Her papa was an earth wizard and her mama a water witch. So even though she was bonded to earth, she still loved the lake."

Of course Zaira wouldn't remember. She was two years younger than Nolan. She must have been two or three when their mama died.

"I'm sorry for your loss," I murmured.

She looked back up at me, her eyes soft. "I'm sure the boys have a harder time with it. They were old enough to really remember her."

I met her gaze. "That doesn't make your grief any less real."

She blinked quickly. "Thank you for saying that."

So much for small talk. Time to move to a safer topic of conversation. And fast. "So, what do you love about being on the water?"

I decidedly did *not* love being on the water. The rocking of the boat was making me nauseated, and I tried hard not to peer into the blue depths below me, imagining how far down it went. I could swim, but not very well.

The other boat pulled even with ours.

Zaira leaned back and stared up at the clear blue sky. "It's peaceful," she said. "We're far away from everything that can trouble us."

"What about you, Kyla?" asked Nolan's papa from the other boat. "How do you like the water?"

Birdsong echoed from the forest. I tried to find a balance between truth and tact. "It's lovely. I think it'll take some getting used to."

His laugh rang out over the still lake. "Well, you're Fintan. Fire never did like water."

THIRTEEN

By the time we pulled the boats ashore, I'd gotten a little more comfortable on the vast expanse of water.

I'd also gotten hungry.

"Come on." Zaira grabbed my hands and pulled me out of the boat and onto the muddy beach. "We're a half mile from home."

Nolan's papa waved us off. "Go on, children. Hogan and I will take care of the boats."

Zaira led us down a quiet forest trail, and Aidan and Nolan took up the rear. The air smelled fresh and clean, and every so often, a toad jumped across the path and disappeared into the underbrush.

"So," Aidan said as he came alongside me, "Nolan didn't tell you about me? Nolan, I'm hurt!" He clutched his hand to his chest and staggered forward dramatically, like his heart was cracking in two.

I chuckled, but another twinge of annoyance shot through me. "Nay, he didn't," I said. "And he ought to be roundly flogged for it if you ask me."

Nolan hung his head in mock shame, but I thought I detected a little bit of genuine regret in his eyes. "I told you I had brothers!"

"What about me?" Zaira asked, threading her arm through mine.

I grinned at her, pleased at how quickly she'd grown comfortable with me. "Aye, he did mention a younger sister."

She stuck her tongue out at Aidan. "He loves me more."

Aidan gave chase, and Zaira let go of my arm and bolted into the forest, shrieking.

Nolan padded forward until he was walking alongside me. "You doing okay?"

I nodded. "We'll have things to talk about later."

"I guess that means I'm in trouble?"

"It means I want to know why you've told me this little about your life when we've known each other so long." I stopped and turned toward him underneath the long, sloping branches of the cedar trees. "Save Breanna, you're my best friend. I want you to feel like you can trust me. It hurts that there's so much I don't know."

His shoulders slumped. "I do trust you. That's why I brought you to see them. It's just . . ."

"Just what?" I crossed my arms. I wanted to give him the benefit of the doubt. I really did. But an ugly, choking sort of feeling spread through my chest whenever I thought about how he'd never told me he had an *identical twin*.

He heaved a sigh. "Papa doesn't really trust the Fintan. Not the council, anyway. He only grudgingly started letting us go to the festival. He's okay with it now, but the day we met, I'd stolen a coin from his purse to buy my ticket. And he's never so relieved as when the clan moves out of Orivesi to tour another county."

Blood raced in my ears. What was he saying?

"So, when we were kids, the idea of bringing my two worlds together . . . terrified me. I was afraid of what I would see in Papa's eyes if I told him my best friend was a beautiful Fintan girl. As I've gotten older, I think I understand him better. He's . . . not afraid of the Fintan. He just knows that fire runs in our veins and we have to pretend that it doesn't, because we're outsiders. He's seen firsthand the heartbreak of leaving to make a new life outside the clan. So he hoped to be able to keep us away from the Fintan. But I had a mind of my own, and it's too late to change that."

I swallowed.

"But," he continued, "even once it seemed alright to let my two worlds meet, the timing never felt right. Because I was afraid of this conversation. I didn't know how to tell you any of this."

"You can always tell me anything," I whispered.

He hung his head. "I know. I shouldn't have kept it from you. And when I was young—"

Aidan and Zaira bolted back onto the path in a flurry of laughter, and Zaira pulled up short.

"We interrupting something?" she asked in a teasing voice.

Nolan flapped his hand at her. "Shut up, Zare." But his eyes sparkled, and she seemed to take no offense.

As we continued down the path toward the farmhouse, I tried to process everything Nolan had said.

I'd known he didn't like talking about his family. It wasn't fair of me to object to that after so many years. But my heart still shrank from the truth that *I hadn't even known he had a twin.* That thought spun over and over in my head like the endless running of a stream.

What else was he hiding from me?

A clearing opened up in front of us, and I blinked to take it all in. A cozy white farmhouse surrounded by two fields— one with a flock of sheep and the other with four cows—and a lush garden. At the far end of the garden were a dozen fruit trees, and on the other side stood a square red barn.

It looked like something out of a storybook.

I turned to Nolan with a little gasp. "This is your home?"

He smiled. "I'm glad you like it."

We walked past a circular well covered by a mossy roof and then over a set of stepping-stones that led through the garden and up to the front door.

Zaira unlocked the door and led us inside. I blinked against the sudden dimness.

We were in a large room with comfortable furnishings that I ached to slouch into. My backside was sore from the day in the boat. To my right stood a doorway that seemed to lead into a kitchen, and across the room was a dim hallway. Perhaps the bedrooms lay back that way.

It all felt so cozy and homelike and . . . permanent.

A permanence I'd imagined but never encountered. The clan was always camping and breaking camp, always moving on or preparing to do so. Often, we returned to the same campsites, but we never settled down for good. I loved that life—the novelty, the adventure.

But what the Malones had? That seemed like a pretty good life too.

"What do you think?" Nolan squeezed my hand.

I grinned at him. "I think I need to sit in one of those chairs."

He laughed aloud and beckoned me forward. "Be my guest."

I took a step, then froze as the floor creaked underneath me.

"It's just the old wood," Zaira said. "It creaks. Don't worry about the noise."

Though I vaguely wondered if the floor was about to collapse, I stepped forward gingerly, mincing my way toward a chair with the fattest cushions I'd ever seen.

We kept our own furniture as small as possible—a necessity when the encampment moved every month or two.

I sat down on the cushioned chair and then leaned back into its embrace, my eyes widening. I was sinking into the softness like an animal caught in a trap.

Nolan and his siblings burst into laughter.

"What?" I demanded. But I didn't scramble up to try to salvage my dignity. Nay, I was far too comfortable for dignity.

Heavy footsteps approached the cottage from the outside, and a moment later, the door opened, and Nolan's papa and older brother walked in.

"What's so funny?" asked Nolan's papa, a good-natured smile on his face.

"Kyla's never sat in a real chair before," said Nolan.

His papa chuckled. "Nay, I expect not. Everything's lightweight in camp. Makes it easier to move."

I wasn't sure I could move if I tried. The long day had exhausted me, and it felt like I'd come to rest in a cloud.

"Hogan, Zaira," Nolan's papa called, "come help in the kitchen."

Hogan and Zaira trailed behind him, leaving Aidan, Nolan, and I alone. A moment later, the sound of flowing water in the kitchen caused me to tilt my head, but I didn't ask. Between the boat and the comfortable chair, I'd already shown too much of my ignorance for one day. It was probably a spigot of some kind. Terra Market had those.

Aidan crouched on the floor and looked up at me. "So, Nolan says you dance in the show?"

"Aye. Just in the troupe for now. My older sister's the Phoenix, but she's retiring. Auditions are soon."

His jaw dropped. "You're going to be the next Phoenix?"

I sighed, the breath coming from deep in my stomach. "I hope so. The competition's fierce." Shayla's face flashed in my mind.

"I bet," he said. "Surely everyone wants it."

"Not everyone," I said. "But . . . enough of them."

"You'll make it," Nolan declared, striding up beside me and nestling into the chair next to mine. "I have no doubt."

"Oh, I have plenty of doubts," I said. "But, as long as it's not Shayla, right?"

He snorted.

"Who's Shayla?" Aidan asked.

I groaned. "My cousin."

"She's the worst," Nolan added.

"Oh, what'd she do?" Aidan leaned forward and rested his chin in his hands.

I sank deeper into the chair. How could I explain what had happened between Shayla and me, when I didn't fully understand it myself? "It wasn't one big thing. Not at first. It was a lot of little things that added up over time. When we were eleven or twelve, she started pushing me away. And then one day she told me we weren't friends anymore. And she's been a raging"—I glanced toward the kitchen—"brat ever since. She wants to make sure she's better than everyone else and that they know it. And she has a particular dislike for me."

Aidan tilted his head. "Do you threaten her?"

I squinted down at him. "What do you mean?"

"Does she feel inadequate around you, do you think?"

I shook my head. "I don't think it's anything like that. We used to be friends. We grew apart once I started spending more time practicing—"

Nolan nudged me hard, and I fell silent and looked at him, confused.

He shook his head slightly.

Aidan's eyes narrowed. "What?"

I wracked my mind. What did Nolan not want me to say?

"When I started spending time doing other things," I finished, my cheeks hot. It was a stupid way to finish the sentence. Aidan would know we were hiding something. Before he could push further, I blurted, "So, tell me about you. What does Nolan's mysterious twin brother do with his time?"

He raised an eyebrow, and I knew that he saw through my trick, but he didn't call out my transparent effort to change the subject. "Oh, I'm training to be a blacksmith," he said. "With Nolan. He and I are going to run Papa's smithy someday."

"Are you, now?" I turned my head to face Nolan. "When were you going to tell me about that ambition?"

He shrugged. "You knew I was learning to be a blacksmith."

The cold feeling in my stomach had turned into a block of ice. I hated how little I seemed to know about him. Maybe I was being oversensitive. I hoped so.

But I looked at Aidan. "What do you like about blacksmithing?"

His eyes lit up. "I like the fire. We're not supposed to use it. Not the way the Fintan do." He glanced down at his hands. "But fire awakens my blood. Makes me feel alive. And in a smithy, I'm around fire all the time. I can't do the work without it."

My heart went out to him. How cruel it seemed to keep someone of Fintan blood from practicing fire. Even the women were taught the most basic fire magic—two elementary techniques for extinguishing fire, and how to keep an existing spark strong and contained—though we weren't technically allowed to *use* those skills except in the direst of emergencies. We girls weren't supposed to know how to summon fire from the air, but if we had a spark, we could fan it to life if we had to.

The flames were in our blood and marrow.

"I'm glad you've found something that makes you feel alive," I said.

My thoughts carried me away. *Something that makes you feel alive.*

Did dancing make me feel alive? I was good at it. I succeeded, surpassing most of the others around me in skill. But it didn't bring me to life.

It made me tired.

I was sure Breanna got tired when she danced, too, but her eyes were bright at the end of practice—and especially at the end of a show.

I felt like that when I practiced magecraft.

But I shook away the thoughts. They were far too brooding and introspective for mulling over in this moment.

So I asked, "What's it like, living out here on a farm?"

Aidan started talking about early morning chores, and working with the earth wizards they employed, and the joy that came with being close to the land. I half-listened—my mind kept trying to return to that all-encompassing question: *Does dancing make me feel alive?*

Breanna's words rang in my head. *Don't let them trap you.*

Zaira poked her head through the doorframe. "Dinner's ready!"

I struggled to push myself up out of the chair and tumbled out of it, slumping to the floor. *How graceful. I've definitely moved like a dancer today.*

"It smells great!" I called to Zaira, scrambling to my feet

She grinned shyly at me and then ducked back into the kitchen.

Nolan beckoned me ahead, through the doorway, and I walked into the kitchen. In the corner, near a large window overlooking the fruit trees, sat a round table that had been set for all of us. On a stove on the far side of the room, a pot of soup bubbled, and Zaira was just pulling bread out of the wood-burning oven.

I blinked. How had she baked it so fast? But I wasn't about to ask another dumb question.

She turned around and took in the expression on my face, and her laugh rang out across the room. "We baked it this morning. I was just warming it a little. Tastes better that way, I think."

Hogan and Mr. Malone both reached for bowls on the table.

"Grab a bowl," said Mr. Malone. "And then help yourself to some soup off the stove."

Zaira grabbed a knife and cut six thick slices off the loaf of bread, laying them out alongside the simmering pot of soup. Nolan grabbed two bowls from the table, handing one to me on his way over to the stove. I stepped up behind him.

The smell was heavenly.

When I ladled it into my bowl, I saw it was a thick stew with generous chunks of beef, potatoes, carrots, and onions. I grabbed my piece of bread and followed Nolan back to the table, taking the seat next to his.

The chairs here weren't as comfortable as the chairs out in the main room of the house, but they were still nicer than what I was used to in the camp.

Aye, part of me could get used to this kind of life.

I reached for the large wooden spoon at my place setting and dipped it into the stew. When I ladled it to my mouth, I closed my eyes to savor the moment. It tasted as good as it smelled.

"Jouko's man came by again this morning," Aidan called to Mr. Malone. "While you were at the smithy."

Mr. Malone groaned as he cut himself an extra slice of bread. "What did he want?"

"Same as usual."

"We're not selling your mama's farm, and that's final," said Mr. Malone.

"I told him that, like always."

"Persistent, isn't he?" Zaira said.

"Who's Jouko?" I asked.

"Jouko Koskinen," said Nolan. "Owns Terra Market and half the land in Orivesi. The Fintan High Council rents the festival grounds and the encampment from him."

I nodded, trying to look like I knew what he was talking about. "Why is he so determined to buy the farm?"

Mr. Malone scoffed. "Why does he want to buy everything?"

I tilted my head, unsure what he meant.

"Power," said Mr. Malone. "Power and wealth. If you control the land, you control the earth wizards."

"And the earth wizards make up three-quarters of Orivesi," Hogan chimed in.

"I see," I said slowly.

"Why do you think so many of the earth wizards are impoverished though they're so talented at bringing forth food from the land?" Mr. Malone asked. "At encouraging crops and trees to grow? When they can sense what the earth needs just by touching it?" He sat down across the table from me.

I took a drink of water and shook my head. I'd never thought to question it before. I mean, wasn't it just because they weren't organized like the Fintan were? But I didn't think that was what Mr. Malone was getting at.

"It's because of scoundrels like Jouko and his father before him. The Koskinens have been buying up the land parcel by parcel. Nine-tenths of the land in Orivesi and the surrounding counties are owned by just three families. The earth wizards can't work their own land anymore. If they're lucky, they get hired as wage laborers by one of the landowning families or rent a small plot to sharecrop at an enormous cost. Those are the ones who have enough to eat and sometimes a few coins to spare to treat their children to a spectacle like the fire festival. The less fortunate . . . well, they send their wives and daughters into the markets to make coin any way they can."

I thought of the women in the low-cut dresses at Terra Market and lost my appetite for the soup.

"But enough about the problems of the world," said Mr. Malone. "Kyla, why don't you tell us a little about yourself?"

I took another sip of soup to give myself a moment to clear my head and think. Was there anything about me that would be interesting? "Well, I dance in the troupe," I said. "But I think you might have known that already."

He smiled. "Your mama mentioned it."

I winced. "I'm sorry she dragged you in like that. She gets . . . protective sometimes."

"As she should," he said. "You don't have to apologize. She's worried about you leaving. Worried that you'll get a taste of the outside world and never look back. But I told her she shouldn't be so concerned. Sure, there is much that is wonderful about the outside world. Land-hoarding scoundrels like Jouko notwithstanding. I'm glad I left because I loved my wife, and I love my children. But the rest of it? I'd give it up to be home with the Fintan."

My mind raced. Something about his statement felt wrong. Different than how Nolan had described his papa. I couldn't suppress the sense that Mr. Malone was lying about something. But I maintained a serene expression and nodded. "Perhaps the council would let you back in if you petitioned."

His eyes darkened. "They will not. When someone leaves, their choice is final."

"That seems unjust."

His jaw softened, and he looked at me with appreciation. "I agree. But it is unchangeable."

Was I so transparent that he could see the plans I'd hatched, the hopes I'd dared to entertain? Or had Nolan told him?

"But I'd love to hear more about home," he said. "Old Eamon's the thane now, is he?"

I took another sip of soup and swallowed. "The challenge is coming up this time next year, but yes, Eamon's thane for now."

He studied me, his intense blue eyes piercing and demanding. "Eamon. He and your mama are brother and sister, aren't they?"

"Aye, sir."

He chuckled. "I'd nearly forgotten. Fancy that. Eamon and I knew each other pretty well back in the day. Never did get along."

Well, there was something we had in common. "I don't particularly get along with him, either," I said.

He guffawed. "Your girl here has good taste," he said, nudging Nolan. Then he turned back to me. "So, is Eamon popular? Or are there a lot of mages interested in a challenge?"

With a shrug, I replied, "I've heard there will be some

challengers, but no one seems to think any real contenders are stepping forward."

"Hmm. Has Eamon been practicing the duels to prepare for the challenge?"

An odd line of inquiry. I suddenly didn't want to be here, in his house. It felt like Mr. Malone was trying to get information out of me. And that made me deeply uncomfortable. But I was only halfway into my bowl of soup, and I couldn't think of a way to gracefully extricate myself.

I glanced at Nolan, but he was lifting a spoonful of soup to his lips.

"I'm really not sure," I said finally. "We're not close."

"Where's the festival going next?" Mr. Malone asked. "Nolan said you're around for a month or two."

I dabbed at my mouth with the napkin. "Two months," I said. "And then on to Kuhmo."

"Oh, really? Kuhmo is less than a day's ride on horseback. I expect you and Nolan can see each other on occasion while the festival's there."

Hope fluttered in my chest, and my discomfort ebbed. Was Mr. Malone supportive of Nolan and our budding . . . whatever it was? Not a relationship, exactly. But we weren't just friends either.

"Will you be back here this time next year, do you think?"

My attention snapped back to Mr. Malone, and that uncomfortable feeling crinkled in my chest again.

Why was he so interested in the inner workings of camp if he claimed they would never readmit him?

"Um . . ." I replied. "I don't know that they've announced plans that far in advance yet." I grasped at something to change the subject. "I hope so, though. I always welcome a chance to spend time with Nolan. And I've so enjoyed meeting everyone today." I smiled at each of them in turn, and Zaira gave a wide-mouthed grin. "Thank you for welcoming me into your home."

"Please come back," Zaira said. "It's been so fun to have another girl around. Usually I'm stuck with the boys all day." She wrinkled her face and stuck her tongue out. "And they always smell bad."

Nolan scowled and swatted half-heartedly in her direction. "We do not."

"That's what you think." She flipped her hair behind her shoulder. "But that's because you're so used to smelling yourself all the time."

I chuckled but decided it was best not to intrude on this sibling squabble. The lighthearted banter continued, and as the sky outside turned pink and orange, I pushed back from the table. "This has been wonderful," I said. "I've enjoyed every minute. But I'd best get home now, before Mama starts to worry too much about me."

Nolan jumped to his feet, the legs of his chair making a scraping sound against the wood. "I'll walk you home."

I gave him a shy smile, phoenixflies fluttering in my stomach. Why was I nervous? I chided myself. This was Nolan. Aye, there was something between us—something wonderful and indiscernible that I couldn't quite put my finger on. But he was still my best friend. The boy I'd grown up running through the festival with.

Why did romance make something that had once been so comfortable feel tingly and strange?

I liked it—more than anything I'd ever liked before. But there was a sort of loss with it too. I didn't want this attraction between us to ruin the easy friendship we'd always had. The joy and sadness danced a bittersweet waltz.

Zaira got up to give me a hug goodbye, and then Aidan and Hogan jumped up from the table to join us, enveloping me in a group hug that felt like home.

I didn't want to leave the Fintan. Not for anything. But I couldn't deny that my heart pulled toward this family too.

I extricated myself from Nolan's laughing siblings and

walked toward the exit. When I reached the threshold, I turned and waved. Then Nolan opened the door, and we stepped out into the cool evening air.

I closed my eyes and let my senses take it all in. The feel of humidity thick on my skin, the croaking of the frogs in the nearby pond, the musky smell of the animals. "It's beautiful," I whispered.

He slung his arm around me as we walked. "I'm so glad you like it. And I told you my family would like you!"

I sighed. "Zaira seemed to, I think. The others were harder to read."

"They loved you," he said. "I know my papa was a little . . . intrusive with his questions at moments, but I promise you that's just how he is. He approves."

"Well, that's good. My papa does too. My mama . . ." I groaned. "Well, we're just gonna have to give that time."

FOURTEEN

Nolan kissed the top of my head when we reached the edge of camp. We lingered there for a moment amid the phoenixflies and the dusky twilight stars and the rapid beating of our hearts, and then I murmured a good-bye. Nolan turned away, heading toward the creek to return home, and I weaved between the tents of the encampment. So much confusion every way I turned. The crushing sense that I would have to choose between the people I loved most.

When I ducked through the flap and into my own tent, Mama was sitting at the table, mending one of her shirts.

She looked up at me, and her expression brightened. "There you are! I have news!"

I didn't like the gleam in her eye. "What?"

Then she seemed to take in my appearance—my muddy hem and tousled hair—and her eyes narrowed. "Where were you today?"

I swallowed but tried to keep my voice light and breezy. "Visiting with the Malones. We went boating on the lake."

Her jaw tightened. "I see. And you didn't think to mention this to me ahead of time?"

"Oh, I told Papa yesterday," I said. I hated to throw him under the cart like that, but it was the truth. And it might save me from the worst of the tongue-lashing Mama was about to give me.

She shook her head. "Your papa is being foolish by encouraging you to spend time with that boy." Then she straightened and laid her mending down on the table. "But come, sit down."

My shoulders tensed. Mama should be angrier than this. Something was up. But I took six steps forward and sank into the wooden chair across from her. It felt so stiff after the cloud-soft chair that had enveloped me at Nolan's house.

"I've been talking with Caolinn."

My nose wrinkled. "Liam's mama?"

Then it dawned on me. The gleam in Mama's eye. Her cheerful demeanor. And . . . Liam's mama. Mama didn't dislike Caolinn, but they weren't close friends. Weren't even really friends at all.

But Liam was my age. Already two years into his mage training. A good Fintan boy.

"Mama, no," I said.

She held up her hand. "You don't even know what I'm going to say."

I shoved back from the table. "But I *do* know. And Liam and I are friends. I like him. But not like that. And he doesn't have eyes for me either."

An image of Liam sprang to my mind. He was three inches taller than me with broad shoulders, a strong jaw, and red hair like mine. Not unattractive. And very kind. He'd make a good husband to one of the other girls. Aislinn, I hoped.

But not for me. He and I had never had those kinds of feelings for each other. And I certainly wasn't going to steal him from Aislinn.

She shrugged. "You can't be sure of that. And things change. Your papa and I were talked into our match by our parents. And we've been very happy all these years."

I clenched and unclenched my fists. "This is not something I will entertain. And if Caolinn had talked to Liam before she talked to you, she'd know it isn't something he'd entertain either."

Mama's expression turned pleading. "Just hear us all out. We're going to have Liam and his parents over for dinner next week, after the Phoenix audition."

I ground my teeth so hard they hurt. "You may have whoever you'd like to dinner," I said. "But you cannot make me marry Liam. You know me better than that. And I won't hear of a betrothal on my seventeenth birthday. Not to anyone."

Mama studied my face. "Not even to Nolan?"

"No!" I cried, throwing out my arms. "I don't want to marry anyone right now, Mama. I want to dance as the Phoenix for a long time before I'm married. Before I get pregnant like Breanna and have to give it all up." My voice caught.

Mama crossed her arms. "We should all be very happy for Breanna."

I stared at her. Of course I was happy for Breanna. I was excited to meet my new niece or nephew. But Mama hadn't seen Breanna's tears. Hadn't heard the desperate confusion in her voice. Breanna wouldn't have shown Mama any of that. She'd chosen to confide in me.

Because Mama wouldn't understand.

I sighed. "We're all very excited about the baby, but I don't want to be pregnant a year from now. Breanna's twenty. And I might want to wait even longer than she did."

"If you wait too long, you'll have fewer men to choose from. Not even that Nolan boy will wait forever."

I wanted to retort that I had a whole world of men to choose from, but that wasn't what Mama wanted to hear.

"And," she continued, "if you start rumors by running around with a boy from the outside . . . well, you know how people talk."

I raked a hand through my hair. "*Why* does that matter so much to you?"

She pursed her lips. "Because, my dear, you may find that

your marriage options narrow dramatically faster if people think you're involved with Nolan in an improper way."

I gave a hiss of frustration through my teeth. "I told you we've never even kissed."

She held up her hand. "And I believe you. But that doesn't mean rumors won't grow."

"I don't care," I whispered. Then I turned around and stalked into my partitioned-off room.

"Kyla," Mama called after me, but I ignored her. I flopped onto my bedroll, still wearing my muddy clothes.

How could she think that she could choose the man I'd spend the rest of my life with? Though the clan limited us, kept us confined in so many ways, refused to give us the same education they gave to boys, we were free to choose our own husbands. And most girls married at eighteen or nineteen, but we were also free to delay marriage as long as we saw fit.

And I saw fit to delay it a long time. My fingers tangled in my hair. Marriage could wait. My dreams couldn't.

FIFTEEN

I tossed and turned, unable to sleep even as last light faded from the sky, leaving our tent in darkness.

I waited, counting forward, counting backward, breathing slowly, trying to calm my racing heart.

And still I lay awake.

Finally, I slipped on my sandals, got up, and peeked into the main room. All was still. From Mama and Papa's room, I could hear Papa's gentle snores. I snuck across the hard-packed dirt floor and through the tent flap into the open air.

It had gotten chillier, but I still sensed the humidity when I sucked in a deep breath. The torches burned throughout the encampment, so I knew it wasn't midnight yet. I wrapped my arms around myself and turned to walk . . . where, I didn't know.

But I wanted to get out of camp. Sit somewhere peaceful. Collect my thoughts. My feet scuffed along the gravel, and then I was on a familiar dirt path, headed toward the creek.

My jumbled-up thoughts bounced around in my head, and I tried to untangle them one at a time. I certainly wasn't going to let Mama dangle me as a prize for Liam's family. Especially not when my heart was with someone else.

Nolan's blue eyes and sandy hair flashed in my head, and I smiled. Couldn't help it. It welled up from the very core of my being.

But I didn't know for sure that Nolan was my future either. And there was no reason I needed to be sure of any of it. Eternal flame, I was sixteen. Why Mama wanted to push me into a decision I wasn't ready for, I couldn't fathom.

I reached the edge of the trees and halted, peering into the darkness. Something about the deep blackness of the forest at night unnerved me, but I squared my shoulders and glided into the cover of the trees. I knew enough magecraft to walk alone without fear of wild animals or a man making violent advances. An adequate defense—enough to scare off an assailant—would only take a moment of focus, a whispered word, and a flick of my hand.

But still, I counted my steps, hoping I'd reach our spot by the creek soon. For some reason, I knew I'd feel safer there, in a familiar place where I'd spent so many hours with someone I cared about.

I wasn't disappointed. As soon as the faint light of the moon glittered off the rushing water, a wave of relief overcame me. I slouched over to the big rock on the bank and sat, crisscrossing my legs beneath me. Closing my eyes, I imagined myself dancing, launching through the steps to Scarlet Moon perfectly, hitting every beat, moving with graceful fluidity across the stage. And then adding a flare of magecraft at the end, solidifying my victory over Shayla.

The tiniest tinge of guilt nipped at the edge of my mind, but I pushed it away. I wasn't technically cheating, and *Shayla* had tried to injure me. I wouldn't feel bad.

Especially not if I won.

Out of the corner of my eye, the bush caught my attention—the one I'd accidentally set on fire a few days before. Even in the faint light that trickled down through the treetops, I could see its blackened branches.

Could I weave the fire in and among them this time? As I thought about it, a spark floated just above the bush, and I drew back. I'd . . . caused a spark just with a thought. That was a first for me. My magecraft was getting stronger.

I raised my head, prepared to clench my fist and

extinguish the ember. But I hesitated, staring at the bright orange firefleck illuminating the night. I didn't want to quell it. I wanted it to somehow light my path, showing me the way forward through all of the confusing choices people were throwing at me.

So I let it hover above the bush another moment longer.

The acrid smell of smoke flooded my nostrils, and I frantically inspected the bush, looking for flames. But it wasn't on fire. The ember I'd formed was still hovering in place.

So, why did I smell smoke? I snapped my hand closed, and the light went out.

Tilting my head, I inched away from the creek and out of the trees toward the path, looking around for any sign of fire.

It's probably just a bonfire.

But even as the thought crossed my mind, I knew I was wrong. The smell was wrong. Wood was burning, yes. But not *just* wood. I searched the sky for smoke and just barely detected it billowing up toward the sky in the distance, dark black against the stars.

Then I heard the scream, and my heart froze in my chest. It was far away, but it sounded . . . desperate. I looked down at my hands.

Would the quellers get there in time? If I started running now, would I get there first?

What would they say if they found out I knew the kind of magecraft necessary to extinguish an out-of-control blaze? And *did* I even know the magic well enough to do it?

I shoved the thought aside and started running. It didn't matter. A raging fire was deadly. I'd never forgive myself if someone died when I could have tried to save them. The gravel crunched beneath my sandals as I settled into the fastest jog I could reasonably sustain.

Another scream, and then a deeper voice yelled. I kept running. Another five minutes, and I could hear the crackling of the fire. It sounded angry, like it was looking for someone to devour. And then, behind me, I heard the sound of hoofbeats.

The quellers.

I jumped off the road and ducked into the shadow of the trees.

Ten seconds later, the horses and wagon rushed by me, five quellers crouched in the back of the wooden cart.

The tension drained from my body. They'd arrived in time. They would save the people. I wouldn't have to reveal my magecraft yet. Not before I was ready.

I swallowed and looked down at my hands and then back up toward the smoke. The fire was just over the crest of the hill. I crept forward through the trees toward the hilltop. When I reached it, I crouched behind a tree to look down at the blaze.

In a clearing at the base of the hill, a wooden structure was burning. But not a home, like I'd expected. No . . . this seemed like maybe a barn? A storehouse? Beyond the fiery building, three others, identical to it, stood in somber silence, as if they were waiting for an ember to jump free of the fire and set them ablaze too.

Thank the eternal flame the quellers arrived before I did. This blaze was too large for me to put out on my own without resorting to dangerous, volatile tactics that I'd heard some of the boys talking about but hadn't practiced myself.

The quellers had jumped free of the wagon and were standing in a circle, positioned roughly equidistantly around the perimeter of the barn. As one, they reached one hand out toward the fire and the other up above their heads. I couldn't hear them over the crackling of the flames, but I knew what they were about to say.

"*Brú,*" I whispered along with them.

They brought their raised hands down in a sudden movement. "*Bás,*" I murmured.

The fire shrank, the flames flickering more slowly.

The quellers raised their hands again. *"Brú,"* I whispered, as if I were taking part in the sacred magecraft.

When they brought the pressure of the quelling magic down upon the blaze, the flames stuttered, growing smaller again.

A third time. *"Brú. Bás."*

This time, the fire vanished, the flames extinguished in the space of a breath.

I backed away. The quellers would stay for another hour, inspecting the ashes for any remaining live embers and searching for any sign of how the blaze had started, but I couldn't be seen here, lest anyone speculate that I'd started the fire. Especially if there was an arsonist on the loose. I shivered at the thought and slipped away deeper into the forest, away from the quenched blaze.

I followed the road back home but kept off to the side, obscured by the trees, where I was unlikely to be seen and still less likely to be recognized.

Life had grown so complicated since we'd returned to Orivesi.

The torches were extinguished by the time I made it back to camp. I weaved through the tents as silently as a shadow and hesitated when I reached my own home, holding my breath and listening for any movement.

I heard nothing except the gentle buzz of Papa's snores. I slipped through the tent flap and back into my room, lying down on my bedroll. No more sneaking out for a while. I'd gotten away with it. This time. But if I had any hope of becoming Phoenix, I needed to be more careful.

Mama was right—the Fintan did talk. And her nagging could easily become the least of my concerns.

SIXTEEN

"**P**oint your toes!" Breanna called.

I extended my leg into a graceful arabesque and tossed the double-headed wand in the air, letting it spin three times before I caught it.

I'd been practicing for twelve hours—first by myself before group practice, and now with Breanna coaching me. The smell of sweat in the practice tent was overpowering. My right toenail was bleeding, and my thighs had never hurt so badly in my entire life. But this was my sixth run-through of Scarlet Moon with Breanna. Twice, I'd executed the steps perfectly.

Now we were trying to improve my artistry, to help me flow across the stage like Shayla, while spinning faster and jumping higher.

I hadn't shown Breanna the flourish I intended to add at the end. Nay, I'd practiced that this morning in the quiet hours, before anyone else had come to the dance tent.

And I was sure that I knew exactly how to add the shower of sparks without raising suspicion. It was in the technique of my arm, flicking it a little wider and higher than I needed to at the same instant I breathed the word and let the magic pulse through my fingertips.

"Relax your fingers!"

I bit the inside of my cheek. She was right. My hands were as stiff as sticks. I'd been dancing too long today.

Almost done. I launched into the final and most difficult move of Scarlet Moon, throwing the wand up above me and launching my body into a somersault. I stuck the landing, jutted my hip to the side, and snatched the wand out of the air, holding the pose for an extra beat.

Breanna started clapping.

I turned to look at her, and the proud expression on her face chased away all my doubts. I was ready.

"That was nearly flawless, Kyla," she said. "Except for that one thing you did with your hands. And you could stand to point your toes a little more."

But I read it in her eyes. She thought I could win.

And if Breanna thought I stood a chance, so did I.

I grinned. "Thank you. It felt good."

"Come on," she said. "Let's get you home. You look exhausted. You need to rest between now and the audition."

"I have practice tomorrow," I said.

"Aye." She pulled me into a hug but then jerked away with a disgusted look on her face. I grinned at her. She should have known I was covered in sweat.

"Go to practice or Deirdre will eat you. But don't come in early. Don't stay late. Just get lots of rest. You don't want to go into the audition tired."

She bent over gracefully—Breanna's every move was graceful—to pick up the snuffer. In a single, smooth movement, she lowered it over the torch and snuffed out the light. When she was satisfied the torch's flame was dead, we walked toward the tent flap, her gliding, me shambling.

We broke out into the festival grounds—dead quiet, on this non-show night—and she glanced over at me and chuckled. "Aye. You, my dear, will be doing nothing except the bare minimum at practice and getting rest between now and the audition."

I gestured with my head to one of the tables near the path. "Let's sit a while."

"Sure."

I collapsed on the wooden bench and leaned over the

table. Pain shot through my feet, my legs, my back. "Ugh," I groaned. "I'm used to pain after practice, but I didn't know every muscle in my body could hurt like this."

She sat down beside me, and her eyes sparkled. "You'll feel better when they announce you as the next Phoenix."

I chewed my bottom lip. "We don't know that yet. It could just as easily be Shayla."

Breanna shook her head. "I mean, it's possible, but you danced that so well. And you've been proving to Deirdre how hard you're working for this."

"But Shayla's been proving herself too," I whispered.

Breanna nudged me, and I grabbed at my ribs with a little yelp of pain. She pulled back, her eyes widening like she was afraid she'd broken me, but I burst out laughing.

"I'm sore, not wounded."

She pursed her lips and folded her arms.

Even though the rollicking laughter hurt my tender muscles, I couldn't contain it. "You should have seen . . . the look . . . on your face," I managed.

The corner of her mouth tugged upward, and she joined in my merriment. When I got my breath again, I leaned back, despite my protesting muscles, to gaze upward. A thin layer of cloud cloaked half the sky, but the other stars were dancing in all of their glory.

Breanna followed my gaze, looking up at the vast expanse stretching over us.

"I'm glad you're my sister," she said.

I leaned against her shoulder. "Yeah, I'm a pretty good sister."

She laughed and shoved me away. "Only sometimes."

We fell into an easy, comfortable silence, and then an emerald phoenixfly flitted past my ear and landed on the table in front of us.

"It's beautiful," she said, breathless.

"You never tire of them, do you?"

"How could anyone get tired of them?"

I shrugged. "Fair point." I still found them wondrous.

The phoenixfly took to the air again, fluttering around us before soaring up into the sky, like it belonged among the stars.

I chuckled. "It was disappointed not to find any fire here."

We fell into silence again. I wanted to savor this moment and keep it close, to live in it forever. Away from the dance stage and the confusion about boys and the agonizing decisions about my future.

"Kyla?"

"Yeah?"

"I really am happy."

I looked up at her and smiled softly. "I know you are."

She sighed. "Mama's convinced you think I'm miserable."

I wrinkled my nose. "Mama's trying to make *me* miserable."

She gave a little laugh. "Now *that* I can believe. What's she doing this time?"

"Trying to set me up with Liam Flynn."

Breanna sputtered and then burst out laughing. "You and *Liam Flynn*? Has she gone mad?"

"Mama's just being Mama. Remember when she tried to talk you into marrying Gainor?"

She made a face. "He's twenty years older than me! His daughter and I were friends as children."

"But he was on the council, and that was good enough for Mama."

"Well." She threaded her fingers together and leaned her elbows on the table. "I'm very glad Papa disabused her of that notion before I had to." A soft smile played on her lips. "And very happy with the way things ended up instead."

I finally asked the question I hadn't dared voice before. "You're glad you married Darick when you did? Even now, having to give up dancing?"

The sigh that wracked her body was deep. "Aye," she said finally. "I wouldn't change the way things happened. I love Darick. I love this little one I haven't met. I'm . . . sometimes excited about being a mama. And I was going to have to give up dancing eventually. I'm glad it's for Darick." She rested a hand on her stomach. "And I'm glad it's for this little one."

She wasn't showing yet, but I reached over and placed my hand on hers. "I can't wait to meet her."

"Or him," she said.

I shook my head. "I think it's going to be a girl. And her Auntie Kyla is going to spoil her tremendously. All sweets and no dinner."

A faint smile turned up the corners of her lips. "You'll be a great aunt." She pushed back from the bench and stood. "And a great mama someday, if you decide that's what you want. But don't let Mama rush you into making any decisions. Or Nolan either, for that matter. You just enjoy the time you get to dance. And I hope you love every minute of it."

SEVENTEEN

My nerves flared white and hot the morning of the audition. I woke up nauseated. It was like the first day I'd ever performed a show in the troupe, but even worse.

I'd jolted awake a half-dozen times throughout the night, somehow panicked that I'd sleep through the audition and miss my chance altogether.

Never mind that the audition wasn't until ten in the morning, and neither my parents nor Breanna would dream of letting me miss it, even if I did somehow sleep three hours past my usual waking time.

First light had just begun to caress the land with its tendrils of lavender and mist.

I pulled on a top and skirt and walked into the main room. Papa was sitting at the table, already dressed for the day and peeling a bilafruit.

He smiled at me. "I thought you might be up early today."

I sat across from him, and he tossed me the husked bilafruit and reached for another to peel. I bit into the fruit's pale flesh, enjoying its tangy tartness. "I couldn't sleep," I said around the bite of food. "I mean, I slept. But not very well."

"Nervous for today?"

I swallowed another piece of fruit. "More than I've ever been for anything," I said, staring down at the table.

He laughed. "More than when your mama found you and Nolan wandering around the festival?"

That brought a smile to my face, at least. "More than

even then. Because I knew that Mama would bluster, but you'd support me."

He reached for my hand and squeezed my fingers. "I believe you can do anything you set your mind to. It doesn't matter that the thane wants Shayla to be the Phoenix. Doesn't matter who Deirdre and the council expect to pick. They'll see your drive and your talent."

I wanted to tell him that the other girls were just as talented and almost as driven—that Shayla might even be as driven as I was—but I tried to soak in the words instead, taking them to heart. "Thanks, Papa."

I ate a small breakfast of shucked bilafruit—my nauseated stomach couldn't handle anything else—and then rose and left the tent before Mama awoke for the day. It was just as well. Papa calmed me, but Mama and I were like sparks to a blastpowder keg. If one of us was agitated, it never ended well.

And I was certainly agitated this morning.

A few people were moving about camp as I strode toward the festival grounds. The audition would be held on the dance stage, and I wanted to get there before anyone else did. To have a moment alone, feeling the atmosphere.

But when I got there, Shayla was already onstage, stretching.

A wave of irritation washed over me.

Shayla noticed me and stood to her full height, smirking. "What's the matter, Ky? Can't handle someone beating you?"

I rolled my eyes and didn't reply.

This only served to annoy her more. "What's the matter? Too afraid to speak?"

"Shut up, Shayla."

A wicked smile curved across her face. "There's that temper I remember."

But I couldn't stop myself. "You don't get to be Phoenix just because your papa's the thane. You have to earn it."

She shrugged and rolled her shoulders back. "I don't expect any special treatment. I don't *need* it."

I huffed. It galled me that she was right. She might *get* special treatment, but her talent spoke for itself.

Grumbling under my breath, I turned around and stalked away, toward the dressing tent. She might have gotten here first, but I'd still take home the prize.

I hoped.

The torches were dead, the tables abandoned. I passed by them quickly, but my eyes darted around the festival, trying to take in every detail, to ground myself in the present moment so I could forget the nerves tugging at my chest.

I couldn't escape the feeling that this day would inexorably change my life, one way or the other. If I won, I'd give my life to the role of Phoenix for the next several years—practicing, perfecting my dance, honing ways to add magecraft to my routine without anyone noticing.

If I didn't win . . . I hadn't thought that far ahead. There wouldn't be a second chance. Shayla was my same age. By the time she retired, they wouldn't want to give the role to me. They'd give it to a younger dancer who had more time before she was likely to get married, and fall pregnant.

I swallowed. I had one shot at this. If I didn't win, the best I could reasonably hope for was to dance in the troupe until Mama married me off to a nice Fintan boy. Like Liam. Or one of his awful friends. *Ugh.*

My thoughts flitted to Nolan, and I shook away the creeping despair. It wasn't true. I had options. I could stay and choose that life. Or I could leave to be with Nolan. Or I could leave and go somewhere else entirely.

Or . . . I could stay and try to become a mage. If I could convince the council, somehow.

I sighed as I shoved my way into the dressing tent. Breanna had urged me to not give up on my dreams, but that one seemed so far-fetched as to be impossible. The council had never let a woman be a mage. Not in our three-thousand-year history, if the stories were to be believed.

What made me think I could be the first?

Breanna's face flashed in my mind, and I pictured her holding her baby in her arms. A baby girl, I felt certain.

What options did I want for my niece? Did I want her to someday stand in this same tent, nerves eating away at her sanity because she only had one chance to pursue her ambitions?

I looked around to make sure I was alone and then lit the torches on either side of my vanity with a whispered word. Perching on the little stool, I examined my face in the mirror. I looked tired. And I couldn't look tired at the audition. They had to envision me wooing the crowds at every show. Like Breanna did.

I reached for my basket of makeup and dug out a clean brush and a small bottle of alabaster pigment cream that perfectly matched my pale skin. I poured a puddle of the cream onto my hand and dipped the brush into it, painting it across my skin with long, smooth strokes. I took particular care to blend it underneath my eyes, where the dark circles most highlighted my exhaustion.

When done, I inspected my face. The flaws were covered—at least enough that they wouldn't be seen from stage. Now time to add the drama.

I contoured my cheekbones with rouge and shadow, and then I lined my eyes with dark black paint that I winged outward from my lash line.

Instead of mascara, I reached for a pair of lavish lash feathers. I'd put these on Breanna enough times to know how to apply them, but as I held them up to my own lashes, I suddenly understood why Breanna asked for help before each show. It was awkward to put them on my own eyes.

So I turned my attention to my lips, first lining them and then painting them a dramatic red.

I was almost done when I heard the tent flap rustle. Breanna walked in, wearing a flowing dress that fell to her ankles, just above her brown sandals.

"I thought you might be here already," she said. "Especially when I saw Shayla warming up."

I waved her over. "Can you help me with the lash feathers?"

A soft smile crossed her face. "I'd be delighted to."

She reached for the tub of sticky paste and unscrewed it, dipping a small brush into it and dotting the liquid along my upper lash line. She held her breath as she carefully pasted the lash feathers on, piece by piece.

When she finished, she said, "Now, be careful not to touch them unless you have to."

I blinked. How did Breanna dance in these things? I couldn't see out of my upper peripheral vision, and they weighed against my eyes.

But I wanted to look the part when I auditioned. And, if I won, I'd have to learn how to dance in them eventually.

"You look beautiful," Breanna said.

I laughed. "That's what I always say to you when I help you get dressed."

"But it's true," she said. "You look like the Phoenix." Tears swam in her eyes, but she didn't look sad. Not entirely, at least.

I swallowed a lump in my throat and stood. "I should get dressed."

Breanna nodded and sat on my stool as I shuffled over to the changing area in the middle of the tent and ducked behind the long curtain. I riffled through the troupe costumes, looking for mine.

It wasn't there.

That's odd.

I pulled the costumes forward on the rack one at a time, reading the names sewn inside.

Raicheal. Ciara. Taryn. Mada. Faline.

Costume after costume after costume. Mine wasn't there. Panic pulsed in my chest. It had to be here. I knew I'd brought it back and hung it up.

I counted the costumes. There was only one missing.

"Breanna!" I called, my voice frantic. "Someone's taken my costume!"

A moment later, Breanna pushed the curtain aside and shoved her way into the changing area. "What do you mean?" she asked.

"I've looked three times," I said, my breath coming fast. "It's gone."

And then the answer burned in my chest. *Shayla.* It had to be.

Breanna darted to the costumes and looked through them one by one. Then looked through them again. Then counted the costumes.

"Eternal flame," she whispered under her breath. "Someone's trying to sabotage you."

"Shayla," I murmured. "None of the other girls would do this, and I'm the competition she has to eliminate."

Breanna's jaw tightened. "Let her try." She pressed her hands together. "Okay. We're going to solve this. This isn't going to wreck your audition. Who in the troupe is closest to your measurements? Can you borrow the costume of someone who isn't auditioning?"

I chewed my lower lip. "I'm shorter than most of them," I said. "I think Aislinn and I are pretty close, but she's competing today." Then I shook my head. "But it doesn't matter. I'll borrow someone's. Raicheal is close to my height. I'm sure she'll let me use her pants. And Mada's chest measurements are close enough to mine that I can get away with using her shirt, I think."

Breanna nodded, but the expression in her eyes was distant, as if she were concocting a plan of her own. "That would work," she said, "but the troupe costumes are designed to hug your form perfectly. It would be clear you were borrowing someone's."

"The council won't notice," I said.

"Deirdre will. And you know she's all about making a great first impression." But Breanna's eyes were alight.

Hope flared in me like an ember. "What's your idea?"

She turned to the parallel rack and grabbed her own costume—the Phoenix costume—off of it. "We'll turn the tables on Shayla. You'll wear mine. Let the judges truly envision you as the Phoenix."

A slow smile spread across my face. Breanna was right. Of all the dancers, her measurements were closest to mine. Her hips were curvier, but unlike the form-fitting troupe outfits, the Phoenix costume had a half-skirt that strapped around the waist and billowed out behind. It would cover the fact that her pants weren't made for me.

"Let's do it," I said. "Quick, let's take it back to our tent. I need to practice the dance wearing that skirt."

EIGHTEEN

reanna and I heaved aside the table in the living space of the tent to make more room for a dance floor. Then she had me run through Scarlet Moon twice. The skirt proved only a minor annoyance. Then she stopped me. "Don't tire yourself out," she warned. "You know this dance. Let's do your hair."

I sat at our table while Breanna ran a comb through my hair and began twisting the red locks into an updo. But she left a framing strand on each side of my face, just like she did with her own hair when she danced as the Phoenix.

When she finished, she stepped back with a grin on her lips. "It's perfect," she said. "You'll stand out."

"In a good way, I hope," I muttered. "They might think it an arrogant stunt."

"Better than by standing out for having an ill-fitting outfit," she said. "Shayla chose her sabotage well. The Phoenix needs to be confident and elegant."

She had a point.

If Shayla had thought to undermine me or throw off my focus by hiding my outfit, she would learn that Kyla Brannon could not be intimidated.

I stretched upward and then dipped down to touch the floor. When I straightened back up again, I felt strong. Like a tree with boughs that waved in the breeze but didn't break—even in the most violent of storms.

I could do this.

Mama shuffled out of her room, her eyes bleary. She took

us in with a frown, her eyebrows knit together. "What's going on?"

Breanna flipped her hair. "Shayla stole Kyla's costume to try to mess up her audition. We're turning it around."

Mama eyed us skeptically. "If you say so."

Breanna laughed, grabbed my hands, and spun me around in a circle. "Let's keep you hidden until it's your turn to dance. I want to see the look on Shayla's face when you take the stage."

Breanna poked her head into our tent. "Aislinn's dancing," she said. "You're up next."

"How did Shayla do?" I asked, reaching up to pat my hair to make sure it was still in place.

Breanna jumped forward and batted my hand away from my updo. "Don't touch anything. You look perfect."

My stomach churned. "You didn't answer my question."

She shrugged. "Shayla did fine, I guess."

I narrowed my eyes at her forced nonchalance. "She was flawless, wasn't she?"

"No dance is flawless."

Which meant Shayla's was close. "No need for you to think about Shayla's performance," she said. "If you think she did too well, you'll think you can't beat her. And you can. And if you think she made mistakes, that will break your concentration, too, because then you'll be worried about making mistakes. Just focus on your own dance. You look like the Phoenix. You'll dance like the Phoenix too."

I took a deep breath and cleared my mind. Breanna was right. How Shayla had danced was irrelevant. I couldn't change that.

I could only focus on giving the council and Deirdre a spectacular show. The likes of which they'd never seen before.

"Let's go," said Breanna. She ushered me out of the tent, and we weaved through the encampment and toward the festival grounds. Though we passed a few Fintan in the camp—who cast us curious looks—most of the community had gone to watch the auditions.

We reached the festival grounds, and my heart beat in time to the music. I saw the stage in the distance. Aislinn was still dancing.

Liam sat on the end of the row, his eyes fixed on Aislinn, and I suppressed a smile.

The crowd that had gathered in front of the stage spurred my heart faster. It was a small number of people, no more than eight hundred—we had ten times this on a busy night at the festival—but I'd never danced for an audience in the daylight before. During the show, I couldn't see the audience, and I could pretend they weren't there.

Though I wasn't usually nervous about performing in front of people, I knew that this would feel different, with the pressure so high. Especially since I could see each and every face.

Papa would be in the audience, I was sure. Even Mama had come to watch. My whole world was here, except for Nolan.

And Nolan's family, I decided. They were part of my world too.

Focus, I scolded myself.

We arrived at the back of the crowd just as Aislinn executed the last maneuver, throwing her wand in the air and whipping into a somersault. Her landing was shaky, and as she reached up to snatch the wand, it slipped between her fingers and landed with a *thud* on the ground.

Murmurs rippled through the crowd, and Aislinn's cheeks flared red as she bent over, grasped the baton, and raised it aloft to strike the final pose two beats too late.

Liam's shoulders slumped. He knew as well as I did that there was no recovery from that kind of mistake. Not in this audition.

I felt sick to my stomach for Aislinn. As much as I wanted to win, I hadn't wanted anyone to feel devastated about their performance.

Except Shayla.

But especially not Aislinn. She was my competition, but we were good friends. And she rarely had a bad word to say about anyone.

The crowd applauded politely as Aislinn walked offstage. She kept her head high and her shoulders straight, but I knew she'd burst into tears as soon as she made it backstage.

I heard Deirdre's voice from the table in front of the stage. I couldn't see her, but I knew she was sitting there to judge the audition, along with four members of the council.

"Kyla Brannon," she called.

Breanna squeezed my arm. "You'll do great," she whispered. "I'll follow you up and grab the props."

I nodded and glided forward, putting Aislinn's disastrous error out of my head. If I dwelled too long on it, I risked making the same mistake.

The crowd murmured when they realized I was moving toward the stage from the grass instead of entering from behind the curtain. The murmurs grew in volume when they took in my outfit.

Shayla was sitting in the second row, I supposed since she'd already finished her audition. Her mouth dropped open, and she shot me a look of disgust. I reveled in that look, used it to fuel my determination. Her sabotage would not get the better of me. Not today.

I climbed the stairs, reached center stage, and stood straight and tall, facing the judges. Breanna disappeared behind the curtain.

Deirdre raised her eyebrows at me, but a smile tugged at

the corners of her lips. "Looking festive today, are we?" she said.

"It's a festive day," I said airily.

Breanna darted back out onstage, handed me the fans, and clapped me on the shoulder. Then she jogged down the steps and stood off to the side, watching.

I would make her proud today.

Deirdre chuckled and nodded at me. I struck the first pose.

As the first flowing notes of Scarlet Moon washed over me, I focused on nothing but the sound of the music and the feel of the fans in my hand. I'd practiced this routine until my toes bled and my feet felt numb. It didn't matter that I could see the crowd. Or that everything hinged on this performance.

Nothing mattered except the rhythm of the music and the beat of my heart.

I took the first steps, steady and sure. And then I merged with the music and danced as an extension of the notes flowing from the violins.

From one beat to the next, I danced, unaware that anything in the world existed except for this moment, this tiny sliver of reality.

I was movement. I was art. I was fire.

The first part of the dance came to a close, and I swept off the stage to hand off the fan and grab the baton. Then the violins began singing again, and I burst through the curtain and soared into a tour jeté.

Again, I lost myself in the flowing movement, the cascade of notes that washed over me.

I came back to myself as I prepared for the final move of the dance. The audition had gone well. Better than I could have imagined. But to vault myself beyond Shayla, I had to execute my magecraft perfectly. At just the right moment. With just the right amount of power.

I swallowed. It was almost time for the somersault.

I threw the wand high in the air and jumped, tucking myself into a clean somersault and landing on my feet. When I caught and raised the two-headed wand, I flicked my wrist and felt the sparks surge upward out of the wand as if they were an extension of my own body. They burst into the air with a crackle, the embers drifting around me like phoenixflies.

I struck the final pose, wand held high, hip cocked to the side. A wide smile flooded my face. The crowd was silent for a moment, and then the cheers began, and one by one, they stood to their feet. Deirdre stood last of all, but she smiled as she clapped for me.

If they gave it to Shayla after this, there was nothing I could have possibly done to win it.

My eyes searched out Breanna's, and I swore she was crying as she clapped. But she had the biggest smile I'd ever seen. *You trained me so well, Breanna.* Tears threatened to well in my eyes, my emotion rising to match my sister's. I blinked them back. It wouldn't do to cry. Not after such a triumphant moment. Not in front of so many people.

I met Papa's gaze, too, and he beamed at me, his eyes misty. Even Mama seemed impressed.

I bowed and then turned and walked backstage, the curtain swishing as I pushed through it. Ciara was waiting on the other side of the curtain, and I slapped her outstretched palm. "You're up next?" I asked.

She nodded, her lips pulled into a grim line.

"You'll do great!" I called. Then I pulled up short. Aislinn sat slumped at the back of the tent, alongside the props. Her eyes were red-rimmed.

"Hey," I said softly.

She wiped her cheeks with her wrist. "How'd it go?" Her voice cracked.

"Quite well," I said. "Thank you. Are you okay?"

She shook her head fiercely. "I messed up. At the most important moment in the dance." Her lips trembled.

I walked over and eased myself down to the floor beside her. "I'm sorry. I guess there isn't anything I can say to make it better, is there?"

She shook her head and leaned up against my shoulder. "It won't be so bad," she said, her voice tight. "I can dance in the troupe another year or two and then retire and find a husband. It was always going to go to you or Shayla anyway."

"You don't sound like it's alright," I said.

She hiccuped. "I'm trying to think of anything that will help me not feel so miserable."

"Oh, Aislinn." I kissed the top of her head. "You're a lovely dancer. It was just one mistake at a bad time. We all make them. It could have been any of us."

She sniffled. "Thank you."

I sat up a little straighter. "Let's go. We'll make some chamomile tea. How does that sound?"

She laughed and wiped at her eyes again. "You're just trying to cheer me up."

"I mean, sure. But tea sounds pretty good. I think my nerves might actually be on fire."

"Tea does sound good." Her voice was still weak. But I hoped the tea would take at least a little edge off her misery.

"Come on," I said. "We'll find Breanna and go to her tent. She always makes the best tea."

"What about deliberations?" she asked. "You'll want to be here when they announce."

Outside the tent, Deirdre yelled, "Ciara Murray!"

I glanced up, and Ciara fairly floated through the curtain.

I waved my hand. "There are still a couple dancers left, and you know they'll take a while to deliberate. We've got at least an hour."

She sniffed again. "Okay."

We sneaked out the back, and her eyes trailed down to

my long skirt. "What are you wearing? Is that Breanna's costume?"

I grimaced. "My troupe outfit went mysteriously missing this morning. Don't want to name my suspects, but—"

"It was Shayla," she said dryly.

The musicians struck up the first notes of Scarlet Moon again.

"That's my guess." I chuckled. Even Aislinn, the sweetest of all of us, had no patience for Shayla.

We rounded the tent, and I spotted Breanna at the edge of the crowd.

Aislinn toyed with the ends of her dirty-blonde hair as we walked up to Breanna. "Let's go." I nodded toward camp. "Aislinn could use some chamomile tea."

Breanna turned sympathetic eyes on Aislinn. "Of course, my dear," she said, pulling her into a hug. "I'm very sorry about that stumble."

I thought Aislinn might be about to cry again, so I started walking backward toward the encampment. "Come on!" I said. "Need to get the water boiling quick so we can be back in time for the announcement."

The three of us began the short walk back to Breanna's tent, and Breanna sidled up beside me. "What did you do?" she whispered in my ear.

My brows furrowed. "What—" *Oh. The magecraft.*

"Would you believe me if I said lots of practice?" I murmured.

Her expression could only be described as *nonplussed*.

"We'll talk about it later," I said quietly. "I didn't break any rules."

That seemed to satisfy her, and a moment later she nudged Aislinn and whispered, just loud enough for the three of us to hear, that even if she didn't win Phoenix, the next show we were learning had three solos that troupe dancers could audition for.

Aislinn brightened a little at the news. She and Breanna fell into conversation as we made our way through the encampment, and I allowed my voice to fall silent.

My mind was whirring. Nothing I could do would impact the outcome now. I could only wait and hope that what I'd done had been enough.

I was powerless. And I wasn't sure if that relieved me or just ramped up my agitation.

My eyes drifted to Aislinn. At least I had the comfort that I'd done well. My heart ached for her.

It seemed wrong that there was room for only one of us to advance. That this competition was the pinnacle of our whole lives. That after this, one of us would have reached the peak, and the rest would go home disappointed, unable to hope for an opportunity for anything more prestigious in the future.

I wanted success. I craved it in my blood. But I didn't want my success to mean Aislinn's failure.

And I hated that it had to be that way.

NINETEEN

islinn seemed more settled and at peace when the noise of cheers rang out from the festival grounds. The three of us sat upright, our eyes wide, all traces of serenity disappearing from our faces.

Had the judges reached their verdict already?

As one, we stood and bolted out of the tent, sprinting at top speed toward the stage.

I reached the grassy field first and stopped. Deirdre was onstage, looking around like she was annoyed by something. Shayla was jogging up the steps toward Deirdre.

I continued toward the crowd at a brisk—but somewhat more ladylike—pace. My heart stuttered, taking in Deirdre, Shayla, the crowd. They must have announced.

And Shayla had won. I'd worked harder than I'd ever worked, performed at the peak of my ability, and still lost. Even with the use of magecraft. Disappointment threaded its fingers through my head, threatening to cave in my skull.

Then Deirdre's eyes locked with mine, and she smiled.

I didn't dare smile back. Not yet. Not until—

"There she is!" Deirdre called. "Kyla Brannon, come on up."

Shayla reached the top of the steps and then turned around and stared at me. Distaste lurked there, in her face, but it passed, and she mustered a winning smile.

What the blazes is going on?

I couldn't think of any reason Deirdre would call us both up. Deirdre was exacting, but not cruel. She wouldn't parade one of the losing girls before the crowd. Then an explanation hit me: maybe Shayla and I would have to perform side by side before the judges finalized their verdict. Plastering a smile on my face, I sashayed up toward Deirdre and Shayla, trying to exude just the right amount of confidence.

I climbed the stairs and narrowed my eyes at Deirdre. *"What?"* I mouthed.

She motioned me over with her head, and I hurried to stand at her side. Deirdre turned to look over the crowd. "I am pleased to announce," she said, "that the council and I have come to a rather . . . unorthodox decision."

My stomach churned. *Oh no.*

"For the first time in a hundred years, two poised, talented young women have demonstrated such keen ability that we have found ourselves unable to decide between them. Please welcome our next Phoenixes—Kyla Brannon and Shayla Sullivan!"

The whole world seemed to stop. I understood the words Deirdre had said, but I couldn't wrap my mind around them.

I was the Phoenix.

I. Was. The. Phoenix.

But so was Shayla.

Deirdre nudged me in the ribs, "Say a few words," she whispered.

"What do you mean?" I hissed. This was all happening so fast. What was I supposed to say?

"Just about how happy you are," muttered Deirdre. "You know."

I didn't.

The applause was dying down, so I took a deep breath and searched out the familiar faces in the crowd. Especially Breanna's. And Papa's.

I found him about halfway back, next to Breanna, beaming at me.

I'd made him proud.

I couldn't wait to tell Nolan. But he was on a journey to a bigger market in the next county for some specialized tools for the smithy. We'd agreed to meet by the creek tomorrow after practice. I'd give him the news then.

I kept the smile firmly fixed on my face as I stepped forward. Took in a deep breath. The crowd quieted.

"Thank you so much," I said, and realized I was warbling. My voice was off-balance. But I forged ahead. No time to calm my emotions. "This is a great honor, and I cherish the opportunity to follow in my sister's footsteps and dance as the Phoenix." My breath caught in my chest at the words. "I've worked hard for this."

My eyes found Aislinn. "I know a lot of other girls in the troupe worked hard too. My only regret is that they cannot all be honored with this role. But . . ." I glanced to the side and offered Shayla a smile. "What a delightful surprise that my cousin and I have both been granted this honor. Fintan fire!"

"Fintan fire!" the crowd chanted.

From her spot next to Papa, Breanna nodded her approval. I couldn't wait to discuss this turn of events with her. This day had been so unexpected. Dizzying.

I stepped back, and Shayla moved forward. Her words were similar to mine, without any hint of disappointment or disgust. We'd both worked hard to mask how we felt about each other. Not that it was any secret to anyone who knew us.

Shayla launched into her conclusion. "Thank you to Deirdre, for the wonderful dance training over the years. And to all of you, for all you do in making the festival happen. Fintan fire!"

"Fintan fire!" the crowd intoned again.

Deirdre whispered, "You're free to go."

I followed Shayla offstage and down the stairs in a daze. I was the Phoenix.

And so was Shayla.

Papa bounded up to me and clapped a hand on my back, the grin on his face speaking his pride louder than any words. Mama flounced over and congratulated me, beaming from ear to ear.

She was probably scheming about how this benefitted my marriage prospects. But I let her crow in victory. At least she was pleased with me, for once.

Shayla, likewise, was accepting her congratulations with a serene countenance. I could only imagine the murder churning underneath her smile.

"Come on!" Breanna's voice tugged me out of my thoughts, and I turned to embrace her. "Let's celebrate!"

She pulled me away from Mama and Papa and through the crowd, stopping every few paces to let me respond to the congratulations the Fintan were heaping on me.

"Don't let it go to your head," she whispered. But she was still smiling.

"It's . . . not quite the same," I murmured.

"I know," she said, the smile still on her face. "But I'm thrilled for you anyway."

I pushed further into the crowd, trying to get clear of it so that Breanna and I could slip off somewhere my thoughts could spin. I needed to wrap my head around what had just happened—perhaps we'd go to Terra Market and look at the flowers.

And then I collided with Shayla.

I jumped back. "Sorry," I muttered instinctively.

"You'd better be," she snapped.

My head jerked up. "Can you just relax?" I demanded. "We both won."

Her lips tightened. "I know what you did up there. I know you used magecraft to cheat."

Blazes, Shayla really was angry. She couldn't contain herself.

Breanna's grip on my upper arm tightened.

I shook my hair out of the updo. "Well, that sounds impossible to prove," I said in a carefree voice. "And even if I *did* use magic, it's not cheating. No rule forbids it."

"*All* the rules forbid it," she hissed. "You're not permitted to use it. Ever. You're untrained. My papa could throw you out of the clan."

"I'm sure the council would frown on me using magic, *if* I knew magecraft." I crossed my arms. "But nothing specifically forbids its use in a dance or audition."

Breanna tugged at my arm. "Let's move along."

I shifted to the side to pass Shayla and tripped, falling forward with my arms in front of me. I hit the grass with a *thud*.

Ouch. I struggled to suck in a breath, scanning my body for pain. My frame felt rattled, but that seemed to be the extent of it. *No serious injury,* I thought. *Just a mortally wounded pride.*

I rolled onto my back and looked up at Shayla. She gave a little smirk. She'd tripped me, the little snit. Oh, how I loathed her.

"Are you alright, Kyla?" she asked in her sickly sweet voice. "I'm so sorry! I didn't realize you were still there."

Sure. I narrowed my eyes at her. "Fine. Thanks." Scrambling to my feet, I grabbed Breanna's arm and slipped into the crowd, fuming.

So Shayla had recognized the flourish of magecraft I'd used. Not that she could prove it. Maybe she was just trying to get under my skin.

But I couldn't suppress the niggling suspicion that she was holding out for the right moment to crush me like a trod-upon phoenixfly.

TWENTY

"Let's go back to the tent first," Breanna said. "You need to change."

I looked down at my outfit and chuckled. Blazes, had I been about to browse Terra Market in the Phoenix costume? The strange, exhilarating day really had gone to my head.

"Market afterward?" I asked.

She nodded. "I was thinking exactly that."

Our steps sounded in unison as we hurried back through the festival grounds, weaving between tables and waving at the other Fintan. When we reached the encampment, we ran even faster, tumbling into Mama and Papa's tent with giggles.

"I knew you'd win!" Breanna declared.

"But I didn't win. Not really. But I did, at the same time." My mind raced, and I started laughing again in frantic, short bursts. *What. Had. Happened?*

"You're the Phoenix," she said. "For now, that's enough."

I should be happy. It's better this way. Even if it's Shayla. That two girls receive the honor—that more than one of us is allowed to reach the pinnacle of success. Better, right? Progress?

If only it had been anyone but Shayla.

Breanna moved behind me and unhooked the skirt from around my waist, folding it carefully and setting it on the table. "Go change," she said. "And don't think about Shayla."

I danced into my room, stripped off the black top, tight pants, and dance shoes, and replaced the costume with my looser everyday garments. Even in my excitement, I gave a little sigh of contentment at the feel of more comfortable clothes. I folded the pants and top and carried them out to Breanna.

She set them primly on top of the skirt. "You ready?"

Pointing to my eyes, I said, "Lash feathers."

She snorted. We sat down at the table, and she pulled them off, leaving them on the pile of clothes.

"Now?" she asked.

I nodded, running my hands through my hair and squealing again. I pulled on my sandals, and we darted through the door and ran for the market.

I bit into a decadent snail roll and closed my eyes at the melding of the puff pastry, custard, and raisins. Nolan was not the only reason for me to leave the Fintan and stay in Orivesi for good, I mused with a chuckle. Snail rolls were also unique to this county and a compelling reason to stay.

But not right now. *Definitely* not now. Another smile broke out on my face. Because I was the Phoenix. It still felt surreal.

Breanna selected a snail roll for herself from the busker's tray, and we strolled down the row of stalls, looking at the fresh produce, colorful fabric, and wooden carvings.

At one booth, three earth wizards stood close to each other, embroiled in conversation. Behind them, potatoes were piled high on the wooden table. I heard the word "arsonist" and strained to make out what they were saying.

"Serves him right," the oldest of the men huffed.

"Can't condone arson," responded a heavyset woman, "especially not with the fire folk in the county. But Jouko Koskinen gets what he gets."

Jouko Koskinen. I knew that name. Mr. Malone had said he owned half of Orivesi.

Why do you think so many of the earth wizards are impoverished though they're so talented at bringing forth food from the land? Mr. Malone's words rang in my head. The signs of poverty here were apparent. The glassy-eyed children. The prominent cheekbones of the women in the low-cut dresses. Even some of the merchants, though not all, seemed almost desperate to sell their wares.

If you control the land, you control the wizards.

And it seemed the merchants shared Mr. Malone's distaste for Jouko.

"Just a second," I whispered to Breanna. I stepped toward the three wizards. "Excuse me."

As one, they reared back, their eyes wide. No doubt afraid that a Fintan girl had overheard them. My clothing, face, and hair all revealed my connection to the clan.

"Don't be afraid." I held up my hands. "I've no intention of repeating your words to anyone. I just want to know more about this Jouko fellow. Why everyone seems to hate him so much."

The heavyset woman eyed me suspiciously, but the old man spat on the ground. "Swear by your eternal flame that you'll not repeat anything you just heard to your council or to Jouko's people."

I clapped a closed fist to my heart. "On my life and by the eternal flame."

He regarded me shrewdly. "Why do you want to know?"

My eyes darted around the market. "Maybe I can help. I . . . just won an audition. I'm the new Phoenix."

Something like amusement crossed his face. "It's no secret what the Fintan think of their women. No offense intended, ma'am. But you're a dancer, not a politician."

It felt like a slap, but I maintained my composure. "Then tell me about the arson in these parts," I said, gesturing at the heavyset woman. "What did she mean that Jouko gets what he gets?"

The old man shrugged. "No secret there've been a lot of fires. All of them burned buildings owned by Jouko. Storehouses, mostly. Someone has it out for Jouko. Does no harm to speak of that, I expect. I've no doubt your council already knows. Jouko certainly knows."

"Who would have it out for Jouko?"

At this, all three of them burst into uproarious laughter. I took a step back, almost offended.

And then the old man contained himself. "You've narrowed your list of arsonists down to most of Orivesi," he said. "Now, here. You gonna buy the taters or not? I rent my land *and* this booth from Jouko, and believe me when I say the rent is murderous."

I gave him a few coins and opened my bag to accept three potatoes. Hadn't planned on bringing food home to Mama, but it seemed like the right thing to do under the circumstances.

"Thank you," I murmured, stepping back and returning to Breanna.

She looked at me, her brow arched. "What was that about?"

I shook my head. "Better if you don't know."

If my feet had hoped for a break after the audition, they were sadly mistaken.

The next day, I arrived at practice a few minutes early. My stomach churned as I approached the practice tent in the early morning light. It looked the same as it always did—the dull, off-white canvas unassuming and subdued. But I saw it with new eyes. "I'm the Phoenix!" I whispered, trying to summon all the excitement of the night before.

But something inside me felt . . . empty. Like the thing I'd worked so hard for wasn't enough to sate my restless spirit. I chewed my lip. Half the other girls would kill for this opportunity. It wasn't right for me to feel unsatisfied. I tamped the emotions down. It was time to dance.

As soon as I swished through the flap, Deirdre pulled me aside.

"You won't need to keep working on the troupe dances with the other girls," she said, the torch flickering behind her. "Breanna is going to start choreographing a Phoenix pair dance for you and Shayla. I expect it to be show-ready in a month. We need to have you dancing it in the shows before it becomes clear that Breanna is with child."

I nodded. I could do that. I'd learned Scarlet Moon in a month.

"Also, the council has decided we'll linger an extra month here. That means you'll be performing here in Orivesi."

A little thrill ran through me. Nolan would be able to see me as the Phoenix. And he could even bring his family.

Aislinn ducked into the tent. I glanced around. About half the troupe was here. Shayla wasn't among them yet. If she made a habit of being late, would Deirdre give the whole role to me instead of making us share it?

Guilt roiled my stomach. If only I were sharing it with Aislinn instead.

"Another fire!" Aislinn exclaimed, her eyes wide. "About three miles away, I think."

Something buzzed in my chest. "What burned?" I asked.

Aislinn shrugged. "A barn, I think. Owned by someone rich."

My hands tingled.

Ciara stretched upward and then reached down to touch her toes. "Local arsonist at it again?" she quipped.

Deirdre turned on her. "Ciara Murray, hold your tongue," she snapped. "Such rumors can start infernos worse than any physical blaze."

Ciara snapped back up, startled. "Sorry, Deirdre."

Deirdre shivered, and her eyes fluttered closed. "Just be cautious, children. All of you. Be careful what you do. Be careful what you say."

A shudder ran down my spine. I'd never heard Deirdre say anything like this before. She always had advice for us, of course, in every area of our lives. Whether we wanted her guidance or not. But I'd never known her to seem . . . scared.

Aislinn and I exchanged uncertain looks.

Deirdre caught my expression and held up her hand. "You young ones hardly remember the last thane challenge."

The challenge was held once every five years—any mage could duel the thane for his position as leader of the council. Eamon, my uncle, had become thane almost ten years ago, when I was a small child. Five years ago, no one had challenged him.

Did Eamon face a significant rival this year? I didn't think so, but I didn't pay much attention to council politics. The conversation with Mr. Malone played at the edge of my mind. He'd been quite interested in learning more about the thane and the upcoming challenge.

Ciara opened her mouth, but then Shayla stalked into the tent, her face wrinkled like she'd just eaten something sour.

A cautious look overtook Ciara's face, and she clamped her mouth shut without saying anything. It seemed no one wanted to ask Deirdre for clarification in front of the thane's daughter.

I sank into my troubled thoughts as I waited for Breanna to arrive to start teaching Shayla and me the new steps.

If the earth wizards were right, if someone *was* using arson to target Jouko Koskinen . . .

Goosebumps broke out on my arms. The Fintan claimed

jurisdiction over all arsonists and took the crime deadly seriously. An out-of-control fire put our clan's very survival in jeopardy. Too many, and we risked losing the goodwill of the counties in which we traveled and performed.

I thought of the heart-rending poverty in the Terra Market. If it weren't for the festival, we'd have less than they did. No land. No useful magic with which to coax life out of the earth. How would we survive if we were dependent on people like Jouko, who cared only to line their own pockets?

Nay, Deirdre was right. Ciara's words were careless. If there was an arsonist, he must be dealt with swiftly, before rumors implicated any of the fire folk. And an ill-timed word, like a stray spark, could ignite a deadly blaze.

TWENTY-ONE

"Nolan!" I called as I jogged up to our spot by the creek that afternoon.

"Kyla." He approached me with wide, eager eyes. "How did it go?"

A giddy smile spread across my face. "I . . . won. Sort of."

"Yes!" he shouted, grabbing me by the waist and spinning me around. The gentle breeze ruffled my hair as he set me down. Then he paused, and his eyes narrowed. "Wait, what do you mean, *sort of*?"

I eased out of his embrace and shuffled through the gravel to sit on our favorite mossy rock. Scooping my legs up to my chest, I said, "I'm the Phoenix. But they gave it to Shayla too."

Nolan sat beside me, dipping his sandaled feet into the cool, flowing water of the creek. "You're . . . both the Phoenix?"

"It's happened before," I said, focusing my gaze on a blue-bird's wings. "But not in my lifetime. Not even in Mama's lifetime."

His eyes crinkled. "How does that work?"

"Pair dances." I made a face.

"Huh." A silence stretched out between us, the song of bubbling water and trilling birdsong filling the space. "How do you feel about that?" he finally asked.

"Confused," I said. "If it weren't Shayla, it'd be different."

His hand found mine. "I understand. But I'm happy you get to be Phoenix."

There was something else in his eyes, something like pain. I tilted my head. "What's wrong?"

He shook his head. "Nothing. Absolutely nothing. I'm happy for you."

I scooted back, searching his eyes. And that's when it hit me. "It's another thing that ties me to the clan. Another thing that stands in the way of . . . whatever this is."

He shook his head and cupped my chin. "I'm glad you got what you wanted," he said. "The chance of seeing you more . . . might have been a silver lining if you'd lost. But that doesn't mean I hoped you'd lose."

I threw my arms around his neck. "I don't deserve you."

He dropped a quick kiss on the top of my head. "Other way around, I'm afraid."

Then I pulled away, my confused, tumultuous thoughts tugging at me. "I'm not satisfied."

His brows drew together. "Pardon?"

"With being Phoenix."

"You mean because Shayla won too?"

"Nay." I shook my head. "That came out wrong. I'm happy to be the Phoenix. Delighted. Grateful. And it's okay that there are two of us. Really, it's better that way. It's not fair that there's room for only one girl to succeed."

He nodded, his lips puckered in thought.

I took a deep breath, hoping that what I was about to say next wouldn't come out as terribly entitled and petulant. "But when they announced my name. When I tied with Shayla, after so many people assumed she would win . . . it made me realize I was capable of more than they gave me credit for."

His eyes narrowed. "What does that mean?"

"It means I want to be a mage."

He kicked at the water. "Well, yes. I knew that."

"You know I want to do magecraft. But I want to *be* a mage. For real. We've talked about it over the years as a distant dream, as something to work toward, as something that might be . . . someday. But I want to work hard for it. Here and now. And then I want to prove my skill in front of the council."

He gave a low whistle. "You want to tell the council you've been learning in secret?"

I crossed my arms and stood as straight as I could. "We knew it would come to that someday. It's the only way. They won't train me, and I don't want to keep my skills a secret for the rest of my life. I want to work the festival as a mage. For a long time."

He swallowed, and his jaw tightened almost imperceptibly.

I reached out for his arm. "I care about you," I said. "I want us to be together. That's why I want the two of us to go to the council and take our mage tests together."

"They'll throw you out," he whispered.

"Then that's their decision. And it will make my path clear."

He threaded his fingers through mine. "You're sure you want to do this? So soon after you've won Phoenix?"

I nodded fiercely. "I want to dance as the Phoenix. But I don't want that to be the pinnacle of my life."

He took a deep breath and let it out slowly. "Alright, then," he said. "I'll teach you everything I know."

"We have two months," I said. "The council has elected to stay in Orivesi a little longer." Though why, I couldn't imagine. We'd already been here longer than normal, and festival attendance was dwindling. But that didn't matter. It meant I got to spend more time with Nolan.

He swallowed and rubbed his face. "I'll teach you everything I know in . . . two months." He stood up. "Come on. Let's go down to the old mill, on the other side of the lake. We're too close to the encampment for this to be entirely safe."

"Oh, none of this is *entirely* safe," I said with a wink. "But that's what makes it fun."

The old millhouse rose up from the ground like a solitary tower of an abandoned castle. Behind it, the lake plummeted like a waterfall over a manmade edifice of stone. The earth wizards had fashioned the mill a hundred years ago, with the help of the water witches, and abandoned it when I was a child. Here, the noise of the rushing water would cover our voices, and the trees would mostly hide the smoke until it dissipated.

We hoped.

"Alright," said Nolan. "We work until last light."

We ran through the magecraft I already knew: creating a flame out of nothing, suspending an orb of fire in the air, shaping smoke, extinguishing flames, forming ashes.

Concept after concept after concept.

"Can't we get to something new?" I asked.

"We will," said Nolan. "But you're the only person I've ever taught this to. I'm trying to teach you like Papa taught me. I don't know what could happen if we skip too many steps. And he always focused on repetition, to make sure I was working from solid principles of magecraft."

"We don't have *time* for all that repetition. We only have two months before the festival moves on."

"You're only going to Kuhmo."

"So maybe I'll be able to see you on my days off, but not every day after practice. We need to do this now."

He sucked in a sharp breath through his teeth. "Focus on the fire. On what it looks like in your mind."

I closed my eyes and summoned an image of the eternal flame that we always kept burning, even while we traveled.

"Are you in the maze?" he asked.

I looked around with my mind's eye. I still felt the gentle sunlight falling over me, and somehow, in the distance, I heard the tumult of the waterfall. But I didn't see the mill or the trees. Instead, I saw a strange white wall in front of me.

I looked to the left and to the right. I was in some kind of corridor. The stark-white walls stretched twenty feet in each direction. To my right was a short, squat white pillar, and above the pillar hovered a ball of orange flame. Further to the right stood another white pillar, empty. To my left, I saw two more pillars: one was empty, and one supported a writhing mass of smoke that shifted from shape to shape.

I was *in* the maze. Not looking down on it as if it were a map unrolled on a table before me. I was standing *inside* it, and with my eyes closed, this place was as real and vivid as the physical world.

When I thought of my eyes, I could sense them, sealing me into this strange, new realm. But they felt heavy, like I was half asleep, like I couldn't force them open without a struggle.

"I'm here, Nolan," I said.

There was a long pause. "Of course you're here." It was as if he were speaking through water.

"I'm in the labyrinth." I turned my head left and then right again. "I see it all around me."

Another long pause. "You . . . what?"

"I'm inside it."

"What do you mean?"

"There's a pillar in front of me. And to the left and right. The walls are white. On top of the pillars are . . . manifestations of the magecraft elements. The elements are moving, like they're alive."

"That . . . can't be right."

But Nolan was wrong. It was as real to me as the daylight. In the past, he and I had always described the maze the same way—as something we looked down at from above—but somehow now I'd entered it differently. I turned and walked briskly to the right.

"Am I moving?" I asked.

"You're standing perfectly still."

All the better. Won't accidentally walk into the waterfall that way. Or run into a tree.

I reached the end of the corridor and stopped. Another white hallway stretched out in either direction. The same short, white pillars were interspersed about every ten feet. In this corridor, three of the pillars were empty. Over the fourth, a cluster of sparks danced as if they were flying out of a wand and then floating down to the ground.

A tingle ran through me. Here, in this maze, was the memory of every act of magecraft I'd ever learned.

Even though I could still hear the outside world, inside the maze it was deadlier quiet than anywhere I'd been in my whole life. My footfalls were loud but didn't echo as I walked down the hall.

"What do I need to find?" I asked.

"Remember when you learned to make an orb of fire hover in midair?"

I frowned. That was behind me, where I'd started. I walked back down the hall and then turned left. There it was. Two pillars away.

"I see it," I said.

"Is there space next to it?"

"Aye." I walked up to the empty pillar. "Right beside it."

"Good. Now summon the energy that you used to suspend fire in midair, but don't use the proper word for it."

I focused on the concept of fire suspension, and a bolt of lightning shot from the fire-suspension pillar to the empty pillar in front of me. I jumped back, but when I looked up at the pillar, an identical orb of fire hovered over it.

A thrill shot through me again, stronger this time, like the lightning was inside of me. "I have it."

"Good," he said. "Um . . . normally I'd tell you to look at the bush that's to your right, but you can't see it, can you?"

I tried to remember the foliage around the mill and lighted on it after a moment. "A rhododendron, right? As tall as my waist?"

"That's the one."

An image of the rhododendron in miniature appeared above the pillar, just beneath the orb of fire.

"Next instruction," I said.

"Now, weave the fire in and among the bush, but don't let it touch any of the leaves or branches, and say, '*Moscaí.*'"

I whispered, "*Moscaí,*" and focused on the image of the bush. Bringing the orb down, I wove strand after strand of fire through the branches until it appeared to blaze. But it didn't catch flame.

A grin tugged at the corners of my lips.

"Open your eyes," said Nolan. "If you can."

I fought through the heavy feeling in my physical body, and my eyes flashed open. I turned to look at the rhododendron. Just like in the maze, flames flickered in the bush. But it wasn't on fire.

Excitement filled me. *So what if I do know magecraft, Shayla?*

A moment later, one of the leaves began curling in on itself, smoke dancing into the air above it. I jumped back, falling into the dirt, and the bush exploded in flame.

Nolan rushed toward it, his hands stretched out. I scrambled to my feet and followed him, one hand in the air, tugging on the thick, heavy threads of the quelling magic, bringing pressure to bear on the fire. "*Brú. Bás.*"

It grew smaller, the plant cringing beneath the weight of the quelling. And then, all at once, the fire winked out.

I glanced up at the sky and saw the last tendrils of smoke beginning to drift apart in the breeze.

TWENTY-TWO

I stared at the smoke, my stomach uneasy.

"I . . . can't believe it," Nolan said.

Swallowing, I murmured, "I'm sorry I set the bush on fire again."

When I managed a glance up at Nolan, he was running a hand through his sandy hair. "Nay, I mean . . . you did it, though. On your first try."

"Second try, technically. And I *still* set the bush on fire."

"What happened? In the labyrinth?"

I scuffed my feet in the dirt. "I wasn't looking down at a map anymore. It was like I said—I was *in* the maze. Everything was white. The skills were still represented by symbols, but the symbols were alive, like real flames. They hovered over these short white pillars."

Nolan sank down to sit in the dirt, and I sat beside him.

"Some of the pillars were empty," I continued. "I think they represent magecraft skills I've yet to learn."

"I've never heard of anything like that before," he said.

"Neither have I."

"What did you do? How did you get in?"

I stared at the waterfall, watching the current run over the smooth stones like the most graceful of dancers. "I wish I knew. I was just there."

"And you've never had anything like this happen before?"

"Never. It's always just been like I was looking down on the maze from up above. A white maze on a black background.

But inside the maze, everything is white. Except for the symbols. Those are in full, vivid color."

"Can you go back in?"

"I . . . think so."

He stood up, brushing the dirt off his pants. "Let's use this bush," he said, pointing to another rhododendron a few feet from the one I'd accidentally set on fire. "Go back in. We're going to try again. This time, focus on maintaining your control."

A soft breeze ruffled the trees as I clambered to my feet and followed him past the poor, unfortunate bush and to the next one. A deep breath filled my lungs. I could do this.

I closed my eyes and tugged at the magic. And I was there again, in the maze. Excitement flooded my limbs. It felt familiar. As if the labyrinth had been calling to me my whole life and I'd finally come home. "I'm here."

"Good." Nolan's reassuring voice filled my mind. "Now, do it again."

I focused on the pillar in front of me and the symbol above it—a bush and a flame fused together. Then I brought to mind the new rhododendron and wove the flames into it. It felt so natural.

When I passed my mage test, Shayla would really be jealous.

A murmuring whisper sounded from somewhere deep in the maze, echoing off the walls in a language I didn't understand. I tilted my head to listen but didn't let the voice break my concentration.

The magic was working—I could see the flame melding with the bush in my mind's eye. But something was wrong.

Behind the pillar, cracks appeared in the white wall, fracturing the smooth surface from the floor to the vaulted ceiling. The fissures spread outward like shattering glass.

"Kyla, stop!" called Nolan.

I struggled to open my eyes, but they were too heavy. A cumbersome, throbbing panic settled into my limbs. What was happening?

"Kyla!"

I forced my eyes open, catapulting my consciousness out of the maze and back into the physical world. Flames were shooting upward from the bush, at least thirty feet high. I scrabbled backward, away from the heat that seemed to sear my skin. But then I stopped, and my stomach clenched.

We had to quell it. And fast.

I shoved down every fear and insecurity and pulled the quelling magic from deep within me, pushing it onto the fire. I would bury these flames deeper than Shayla wanted to bury me.

The cloying, choking smoke was thick and black, not like natural woodsmoke. My eyes burned.

What the blazes was happening?

Beside me, Nolan worked, his hands pointed at the fire, his jaw tight, a vein bulging in his forehead.

The flames danced higher, licking upward.

"Die," I muttered, forcing the quelling magic to press against the tops of the flames.

The fire was shrinking. I pushed harder.

And then, all at once, the flames vanished, leaving a blackened ruin where the once-green bush had stood. Ash rained down around us like snow. A few flecks gathered in Nolan's hair.

Nolan stepped back, sweat rolling down his face. "Let's . . . not try that again today."

He didn't have to tell me twice.

The smoke was still curling into the sky, blending with the first hints of evening.

"Let's get out of here," I said, my voice shaking. "The quellers surely saw all that smoke. They'll be coming."

He bit down hard on his lip and nodded, walking around the whole plant—or what was left of it—to check for stray sparks.

"It's dead," he said. "Let's go."

We took off jogging along the lakeshore. "We don't want to be seen," I said. "And the quellers will likely come on this path." I nodded to the forest on our right. "I think we should pick our way back through the trees."

He hesitated. "It's nearly dark."

"Doesn't matter," I said. "Besides, we can move back onto the road once the quellers have passed us."

He considered this and then nodded. A mourning dove cooed in the distance as we stepped off the road and picked our way into the woods. Once we moved beyond the first row of trees, I blinked, willing my eyes to adjust to the dimness. It felt like I was about to walk into a spiderweb—or worse.

"Let's not go too deep," Nolan said, confirming my own instincts. "We don't know what's in here."

I didn't know what I was afraid of. Sure, there were wild-cats and bears in Orivesi, but they weren't aggressive. Perhaps they'd be dangerous to a small child wandering alone, but not two full-grown people walking together.

"Papa says there are dragonbeasts in the woods," Nolan said.

I laughed, but my voice shook. "Those are bedtime stories."

"Had to come from somewhere, didn't they?"

"From the old days. They died out hundreds of years ago." But his words sent another shiver down my spine, and I vowed to be extra careful. Dragonbeasts might not be alive anymore, but wildcats were.

And I supposed even a wildcat could be aggressive if it was hungry enough. Out of the corner of my eye, I detected movement. A tiny animal skittered up a tree trunk.

Just a squirrel.

This was a living forest. Animals abounded. As Nolan and I pressed forward, staying parallel to the path but forging deep enough in the woods that we were unlikely to be noticed, I forced my heart to still every time the crunch of foliage to my left or right shattered the stillness.

Not that the forest was particularly still to begin with. Neither Nolan nor I possessed the gentle magic that bound earth wizards to the land, and *we* sounded like dragonbeasts as we tromped through the undergrowth.

The trees loomed up around us like shadows, and the plant life along the forest floor reached out, thorns tearing at our clothes, fallen logs rising up to trip our feet.

Cold sweat trickled down my back.

Just keep moving.

In the distance, I heard the sound of hoofbeats.

"The quellers," I whispered. "Get down."

Nolan and I ducked toward a pair of close-set, thick cedars, and each of us crouched behind one of the trunks. The quellers wouldn't be searching for us yet—they'd be focused on finding the source of the smoke—but once they realized that there was no fire to put out . . .

They might think we're the arsonists.

Even though I was sure no one would be looking into the trees, I willed myself to stay perfectly still, to not allow even a flash of movement to hint of our presence.

The hoofbeats grew louder, and I could hear the groaning of the wagon wheels. I held my breath.

In a thunder of noise, the quellers' wagon passed by, not hesitating as it clattered down the path toward the old mill.

I waited three, four, five heartbeats and then nodded at Nolan. We crashed through the bushes toward the path that ran along the lake.

When we reached the edge of the road, I bent over, hands

CATHERINE JONES PAYNE

on my knees, huffing in great breaths of air. *Stay calm. Stay calm.* Nolan stood in front of me, gazing back into the woods. His eyes widened.

My heart hitched. "What is it?"

"Wolves," he whispered.

TWENTY-THREE

I slowly turned to gaze back into the forest. Sure enough, eight wolves stood within the trees, teeth bared. I couldn't move. Couldn't breathe. Couldn't swallow.

Wolves? This time of year? They passed through the county sometimes but rarely stayed. There weren't enough deer here to keep a pack well fed.

My eyes traced their shaggy coats. These wolves were too thin. They'd been hunting here a while. And hadn't been successful.

And now they were hunting us.

"Blazes," said Nolan. "Can wolves swim?"

The lake stretched out behind us, but I didn't dare look at it. "Better than I can, I suspect," I murmured.

"If we run, they'll give chase."

The largest wolf stepped forward, growling. We were out of time. My eyes flitted to the forest. We might be able to climb a tree, but I didn't think we could get high enough before the pack reached us. We could try to brave the lake. I didn't think I could stay afloat long enough to survive, but at least Nolan stood a chance.

My fingers tingled. We had to fend the wolves off with magecraft. It was the only way. But the quellers were so close that we were likely to be caught.

My throat felt tight. *I'd rather explain my actions to the council than be torn apart.*

I raised my hands. "We have to fight them off."

There was a long pause, and then Nolan replied, "Let's do it."

The largest wolf leaped forward, and I closed my eyes, finding myself standing in front of a white pillar. Over the pillar floated a stream of fire, spinning in circles. I'd executed this concept once before. That would have to be enough.

I opened my eyes, and the fire flew out of my hand and hit the wolf squarely in the chest. It shrieked, and then the fire enveloped it.

I hardened my heart against its piteous howl. "I'm sorry," I whispered.

Another wolf decided to try its luck, and Nolan beat that one off with a smaller flare that flew past its ear. It shied to the side and then turned and slunk away.

The other wolves, seeing their leader go up in a blazing flame, had begun backing up.

One of them gave a howl, and they turned as a unit and melted into the shadows. But the fire that had killed the largest wolf had jumped to a nearby tree, the flames crawling from branch to branch. Then it leaped to another tree.

My heart hammered. I'd set the forest ablaze.

Nolan pulled on my sleeve. "Kyla, we have to go."

"We started a fire," I said.

"The quellers are close. They'll stop to put it out. They can't find us here."

It went against everything I knew to be right, but if we stayed, we put our lives in jeopardy. I turned and fled up the path alongside Nolan, pleading for the quellers to get back before the flames caused serious damage.

We sprinted until we reached the far end of the lake, and I pulled him to a stop. "Go home," I said. "Get inside as fast as you can."

He squeezed my hand. "Stay safe."

And then he turned and ran in the direction of the

farmhouse. I took off again, my lungs screaming their protest, toward the encampment.

The road forked off, following the creek, and I hurtled up it, my sandals catching on tree roots and stones. My foot landed in a small divot in the ground and wrenched sideways, and I fell forward, landing in the dirt with a *thunk*.

Pain exploded in my hip and ankle.

At first, I couldn't breathe. Couldn't do anything. Then the air came rushing back into my lungs, and I buried my mouth in my arm to keep from screaming.

Searing agony lanced through my right ankle, and I was pretty sure I'd hurt something in my hip too. Or maybe it was my lower back.

I dragged myself to my knees, and collapsed again to the ground.

The quellers would find me here, injured. I'd be taken to the council for questioning. And certainly branded an arsonist, after the blazing fire I'd left in the woods.

"Kyla?"

I knew that voice as well as I knew my own.

I tilted my head and looked up at Breanna.

She crouched in front of me. "Kyla Brannon, what is going on?" she demanded.

"What are you doing here?" I asked through gritted teeth.

"Going out to find Darick," she said. "The quellers went out after one fire, and I saw the smoke of a second, and—" She broke off. And then her voice grew colder. "What are *you* doing here?"

Pain still pulsed in my hip and ankle. "Being injured," I muttered, looking back down at the ground.

I knew her so well that I could *feel* the questions circling in her mind, but she just said, "Do you need help to get home?"

I nodded, managing to roll onto my back. That soothed my throbbing hip a little. And we were almost back to camp.

Breanna helped me to my knees and then to my feet. Well, to one foot, anyway. I didn't yet know if I could put my full weight on my ankle.

She encircled my waist with her arm, helping me limp over the ridge and into camp.

"Come to my tent," she said, her voice stern. "We need to talk. Privately."

I tried to swallow, but my throat felt dry and parched. This wasn't going to be fun. We wended our way among the outermost tents to avoid the eyes of too many people, but this time of day, we couldn't avoid everyone.

"Did you not find Darick?" Liam's mama stepped into our path.

Breanna waved at her. "Caolinn! I haven't gone to find him yet. I asked Kyla to come with me, and we hadn't even gotten out of camp before she hurt her ankle and needed help home."

Caolinn tsked. "You should take better care of yourself, Kyla. Can't have our Phoenix dancing on weak ankles."

I murmured, "Aye, ma'am. I really need to go sit down. Good evening."

Caolinn peered at me with unabashed curiosity written on her face, but we shuffled past her and between two more tents before we finally reached Breanna's.

Breanna helped me through the flap, and I collapsed onto the ground next to the fire, rolling onto my back and letting out a deep groan. A soft floral scent reached my nostrils.

The tent soared above me, its white material soft and dull in the low light of evening. Breanna sat cross-legged next to me. "You're going to explain yourself," she said in a quiet voice.

"What am I explaining?" I asked, still staring up at the tent fabric.

"Where were you?"

I closed my eyes. Should I tell her that Nolan and I

had been out together? Nay, I didn't want to bring him into this.

"Down by the creek," I said.

"Do not lie to me," she snapped. "You were running so fast and carelessly that you fell, coming from the direction of two fires. You reek of smoke. The end of your left sleeve is singed. I need answers, Kyla."

I glanced down at the offending sleeve and saw a trace of black at the cuff. That would need mending. Then I rolled over to face Breanna. My hip screamed in protest, but I didn't care. "Do you think me an arsonist?" I demanded, hurt lacing my voice.

She leaned back on her hands. "Arsonist? Blazes, no, Kyla. Don't even say such a thing."

I relaxed a little and eased onto my back again.

"But," she continued, her voice falling even quieter, "I know you and Nolan have been working on . . . some things the council is unlikely to approve of. Things that might start fires on accident."

Blazes, she was perceptive sometimes.

With a deep exhale, I said, "I put out the first one. There was nothing for the quellers to fix. The second one . . . there were wolves, and I accidentally set the trees on fire scaring them off, and I had to run before the quellers caught me."

"So you left the trees ablaze?" she asked.

I couldn't bear to answer, so I nodded.

"They could kill you for that," she hissed. "Or turn you out of the clan."

"It wasn't like I wanted any of this to happen," I whispered, a tear streaming down my cheek.

"What did you *want* to happen?" She raked her fingers through her hair like a madwoman.

The sigh that wracked my body came all the way from my soul. "I want to earn the right to make my own choices."

"That's not going to happen if you set the forest on fire."

"I know," I said. "It was a terrible mistake. One I will not repeat."

Her lips pursed.

"You're not going to tell them, are you?"

She lay down beside me. "Of course not. I just . . . don't want you to get hurt. Or to accidentally hurt anyone. You don't have the training . . ."

I scooted over and rested my head against her shoulder. "You were the one who told me not to let them take my dreams."

She gave a dark chuckle. "I regret every word." And then she turned fearful eyes on me. "Don't make me regret keeping this from Darick."

"I promise."

Her eyes shifted down to my ankle. "And don't get hurt again. They could always decide Shayla gets to be the sole Phoenix."

I turned onto my side and twisted my lower back, the joints making a popping noise.

Breanna cringed.

Flopping onto my back again, I moved left to right, testing the hip. Popping it had helped.

I shifted to all fours and then slowly raised myself to my feet, the bulk of my weight on my good ankle.

Bit by bit, I put weight on the ankle I'd injured. It hurt, but it didn't buckle beneath me.

It had sent searing pain through me when I'd turned it, but I knew it wasn't broken. Sprained, maybe, but not badly.

"I can dance on it in a week," I said.

Breanna's face scrunched, and I knew what she was thinking: that a week was too soon to dance on an injury *and* that Deirdre would throw a fit when I said I had to miss a whole week of practice.

But a fit from Deirdre didn't worry me. Not when I'd so

recently been worried about the quellers hauling me before the council and accusing me of arson.

I sank into a chair at Breanna's table. I was safe.

My sister sighed heavily. "Come on. We need to get you back to Mama and Papa's tent so you can change. Can't have anyone seeing you with that burnt sleeve today."

TWENTY-FOUR

Deirdre granted me seven blissful days of reprieve from practice, announcing that Breanna would dance one additional week of shows. The thought tugged at me uneasily—what if, during my week off, Shayla somehow convinced Deirdre that I should be stripped of the role altogether? But I scolded myself for the foolish thoughts. Deirdre alone couldn't make such a decision. For a Phoenix to lose her place, the whole council would have to decide unanimously.

I could hobble adequately on the injured ankle, and Deirdre had warned me to keep it limber with slow walks and gentle stretching. So I limped down to the creek each morning to spend every spare moment with Nolan, or to wander the white maze in my mind when Nolan wasn't able to meet me.

After the disastrous incident with the burning bushes, I was afraid to try that particular mage concept again. So when I went down to the creek to explore the white maze, I practiced on things I already knew, doing them over and over and over, hoping to discover some secret to better control the magecraft. Repetition, Nolan had said, was how he'd learned.

On the fourth day, I sat cross-legged on the mossy rock, suspending a fiery orb above the creek. Every few seconds, I whispered another word, and the orb changed color. I smiled. When the magic worked right, practice was really a lot of fun.

A red phoenixfly fluttered through the trees, its wings

struggling to flap. Its flame was going out. It surged valiantly toward the orb—which was now a brilliant shade of yellow. A forest breeze hit the phoenixfly, knocking it down toward the creek, and I moved my hand to send the orb floating toward it. The fire collided with the phoenixfly mere inches above the water. I held my breath. Had I gotten to it in time?

Then the phoenixfly fluttered upward, its wings now the color of a dandelion.

With a whispered word, I created another orb, this one turquoise, hovering in the air alongside the first. Then a third, fuchsia. I levitated the orbs in the air, sending them spinning in circles.

The phoenixfly descended again, flying near the fire. It fluttered through the turquoise orb, its wings brimming in blue-green flame. Then it chased the fuchsia orb, floating through it and then flying around my head, as if it was delighted to now be shining a lovely shade of dark pink. It surged toward the orbs again, dancing through one, then another, changing color time and time and time again.

I laughed aloud. After a few minutes, the phoenixfly grew tired of the game and fluttered away into the trees, its turquoise wings flashing in the shade. "Be safe!" I called to it.

Holding up my hands, I extinguished the orbs and stood to stretch.

I'd certainly improved—something about being in the maze helped everything come together in my mind in a new way—but I feared I was stagnating. That Nolan wasn't teaching me new things quickly enough. And I didn't have time to stagnate. Nolan and I had to pass the mage test before the Fintan moved on to the next county. I wouldn't be able to get enough practice time with him once we left for Kuhmo.

I'd run through everything I already knew a dozen times. Nolan would be here soon.

I bit my lip and sat back down. Blinking, I found myself in the maze. A voice whispered words in a foreign tongue.

I turned to look for the source of the whispers. But there wasn't anyone else in my line of sight. Then, a clear, feminine voice rang out. "Smoke."

That was new.

"What?" I looked around again. "Who's there?"

But the whispers fell quiet, and the voice did not speak again.

I shrugged and looked at the nearest pillar. Above it, a cloud of smoke was shapeshifting, forming first a circle, then a tree, then a horse. I studied it, nodded, and opened my eyes to see the forest glade. With a deep breath, I let smoke rise up from my hands. I sat there for another hour, fashioning the smoke into shape after shape after shape.

Forming smoke wasn't a new concept, but it seemed like the maze had . . . guided me to it. Since the fires, Nolan had taught me a single new magecraft skill—the ability to make shapes, not out of smoke, but fire.

My favorite was a fiery image of a phoenixbird that I brought to life over a bed of ashes.

I accessed the labyrinth and called forth a thin layer of ashes. They materialized in front of the rock. Then, I closed my mind, re-entered the maze, and stood in front of an ever-morphing flame that hovered over a white pillar. "Phoenixbird," I whispered.

I opened my eyes, and a small ball of fire was rising out of the ashes. I splayed my hands, and it formed into a tiny phoenixbird with rippling feathers of flame.

I smiled and waved my hand to whisk the phoenixbird toward me. It turned and flew to me, alighting on my hand without burning me.

"Told you not to do that," said Nolan as he entered the glade.

I jumped, and the phoenixbird flickered out of existence. "I was domesticating it," I said.

He snorted. "You shouldn't practice new skills alone. No

one should. Always safer to have at least one other person with you."

I shrugged. "This one seemed pretty small and contained."

"I know, I know," he grumbled. "You can't resist. Make a pillar."

I closed my eyes, and the white maze flashed in front of me. When I opened my eyes, a small pillar of fire floated in front of me.

"Now a waterfall."

That was easy. I only had to blink, to enter the maze for a fraction of a second, and the pillar reformed itself into a waterfall modeled after the one at the old mill.

"Very good," murmured Nolan.

Take that, Shayla.

A dozen sparks showered out of the waterfall and hit the ground, igniting a patch of grass. I scrambled to my feet.

Nolan pushed his hands out toward the grass, and the flame extinguished. He rubbed his temples.

I clapped my hand to make the waterfall vanish and sank to a seated position on the rock. My confidence flickered.

Nolan's eyes met mine in a long, tense moment.

"I don't know how to keep it contained." The words burst out of me before I could stop them.

He nodded, a deep sigh wracking his chest. "You've always been talented," he said, and then he paused. "And . . . even more so since you've been able to go into the maze yourself. But without control, all that power is dangerous."

I chewed the inside of my cheek. My heart wanted to resist his words, but I knew he was right. What was deadlier than an uncontrolled fire? "And you don't know how to help me control it?"

Agony shone in his eyes. "I mean, *I* know how to control it. I keep a peaceful mind. I focus all my attention on the flame."

"I'm doing all that," I said, though a single doubt wavered

in a corner of my mind. Since Shayla had tried to sabotage me—twice—and been named the Phoenix for her efforts, I'd been pursuing mage training with a tinge of jealousy, a desire for vengeance coloring all that I did. Sometimes it seemed like my power grew stronger when the jealousy was closest at hand.

That probably wasn't what Nolan meant by *a peaceful mind*.

I resolved to set the jealousy aside, to center myself and focus on the present moment. That was how Nolan had always taught me to practice magecraft. It was what the Fintan masters drilled into their mage students.

"Let's go again," I said.

He gave me a doubtful glance, but he nodded.

I took a deep breath, focusing on the steady rise and fall of my chest, on the sound of the running water, on the image of the fiery waterfall in my mind. Then I closed my eyes.

Nothing happened. I couldn't find the white maze. I opened my eyes, my brow furrowed. "That's funny," I murmured.

"What?" Nolan asked.

But I shook my head, took another deep breath, and closed my eyes. Again, nothing.

A suspicion uncurled in the deepest recesses of my mind. Had the jealousy itself been what had fueled my rapid improvement? My ability to access the maze that now meant so much to me? Had my anger brought about my success?

I opened my eyes again and tilted my neck all the way to the left and then all the way to the right. When I straightened it, I brought a picture of Shayla to the forefront of my mind. Of her smirk after the wand had exploded above me.

Of the horror I felt when I'd realized she'd stolen my costume. Then I pictured the flaming waterfall around her, consuming her.

I closed my eyes again, and I was in the white corridor.

Relief tingled through me. I hadn't lost it.

But some part of me still felt afraid. Would this power that brought me success require me to foster darker and darker emotions? Would the price of magecraft be my soul?

I didn't want that.

But I also didn't want to fail, to fade away into obscurity, to realize nothing I'd worked so hard for.

I opened my eyes, blinking against the gentle light of day. The fiery waterfall was growing larger.

Nolan looked at me, shaking his head. "Put it out," he said. His voice was calm, but that vein was bulging in his forehead.

The floating fire grew larger and brighter, and I raised a shaky hand, extending the other toward the flame. "*Brú*," I said. But I couldn't sense the strings of the quelling magic. "*Bás*." I brought my hand down to send the pressure of the quelling magic crashing over the fire. But nothing happened. It was like something in my mind was blocking me from accessing the magecraft.

And still the fire grew.

"I can't!" I yelled. "You do it."

"You have to," he called. "You have to take control of it!"

I tried to calm my mind, to grasp at the quelling magic. But I still couldn't access it. Then I summoned an image of Shayla's smug face.

There it was. Three small, bright-white strands in my mind. I grabbed at them.

The fire flared bigger and hotter.

I tugged on the strands and felt the quelling magic fill me. Then I moved toward the flames, my hands outstretched.

"Die," I muttered. I wasn't sure if I was saying it to the fire or to the image of Shayla mocking me in my head.

Part of my mind recoiled. When had my anger at her become such vicious hatred?

"*Brú!*" I yelled. "*Bás!*" I brought the pressure of the quelling magic down upon the fire, and it sputtered, getting smaller. I took a deep breath, trying not to cough as the smoke tore at my lungs, and pressed the quelling magic onto the flames again.

The fire shrank again, and then suddenly exploded back to life, ballooning outward. I stumbled back.

This wasn't working.

I looked at Nolan desperately. He was on his feet now, trying to quell it, and it wasn't going out.

Panic flared in my chest. Why wasn't it responding to the quelling magic?

I tried again. Nothing. Sweat trickled down my back.

But there was still one more thing I knew to try. Something I'd overheard Liam and Bard talking about but hadn't put into practice.

Instead of extinguishing a fire by putting pressure on it, I could suck out all the air from around it.

It was an advanced magecraft tactic. One I *definitely* wasn't supposed to know of, because it was particularly dangerous. Volatile. If I did it wrong, I could suck all the air out of my lungs and Nolan's—crushing our chests and killing us both.

"Get back!" I waved my hands frantically at Nolan. "I'm putting it out."

He set his jaw but nodded and took several steps back.

I wanted to take a deep breath to prepare myself, but the smoke and heat blazing off the inferno forced my breaths to stay quick and shallow.

A spark jumped off the blaze and ignited a nearby tree.

I needed to do this *now*.

I blinked, landing in the white maze in front of an empty pillar. But when I looked more closely, I realized it wasn't really empty. Something almost like fog hovered above it, starting in a tiny, concentrated ball and bursting outward. But the symbol was faded and transparent—like it wasn't all the way congealed yet.

It would have to do.

I forced my eyes open, took one last breath, and let the magic flow out of me and into the fire. "*Inphléasc*," I whispered.

Please work.

I couldn't look to see how far Nolan had backed away. I hoped that, if this went badly, I'd be the only one to die. That I wouldn't hurt anyone else.

Especially not Nolan.

I pleaded wordlessly with the magic to keep us safe, as if it could hear me. And then three thin wisps of fog flowed from my hands into the center of the fire. Pressure built up inside me, begging for release.

The fog disappeared, but I knew it had formed a pocket in the middle of the flames. I sucked in a breath and then clapped my hands and released the tense, fidgety power in my chest.

The fire imploded, as if sucked into a tiny ball. A moment later, only a small orb of fog remained. It fell to the ground and rolled into a divot in the earth, solidifying into a perfectly round, white stone.

I took a step back, my heart pounding. I was alive.

I looked back, and my gaze alighted on Nolan. He was standing upright, his eyes wide and face flushed.

I exhaled all the smoke out of my lungs and sucked in a breath of clear, cool air. All traces of the fire had vanished. Not even a wisp of smoke remained.

My gaze drifted down to the marble, and I bent down and reached for it, my fingers closing around its smooth surface. It was unnaturally cold to the touch.

I stood back up and let the marble rest in my palm. On impulse, I held it up to my mouth and breathed on it, and it gave off a little steam.

"Have you ever seen anything like it?" I asked Nolan.

He approached me, reached out, and traced the stone

with his finger, drawing back in surprise when he touched it. "No . . . I've used that tactic a handful of times to put a fire out—just in practice—and the fog's always evaporated. It's never solidified like that."

A turquoise phoenixfly fluttered past me, and I recognized that particular shade of fire. *Hello, again.*

I glanced down at the marble and then met Nolan's gaze. "It almost looks like the walls of the maze. The color and sheen is right."

He opened his mouth, but only stutters came out.

What the blazes is going on?

TWENTY-FIVE

The days flowed into each other like the unending current of the creek. Soon, Deirdre declared my ankle healed enough to dance on, so dance I did. Even if it was still sore. The time passed in a blur—dance practice, training with Nolan, laughing with Breanna, and sleeping.

I did little else. But in my few moments of solitude, I often found myself pulling out that strange marble. Studying it. Wondering why it had appeared. I kept it in the pouch with the coal Nolan had given me as a gift.

Two weeks later, Deirdre clapped her hands when I arrived at practice. "There you are, Kyla. No dancing for you and Shayla today. You're both learning the steps beautifully, and it's time to get your hair painted."

A thrill ran through me. Almost every member of the clan had blond or red hair. But the Phoenix was unique. To dance this role, we had to look the part. We had to look like fire.

So the Phoenix's hair was always dyed, always in the same way—the root, dark brown, almost black, like coal. And the rest of her hair highlighted in crimson, orange, amber, and gold—the colors of the eternal flame. It was a symbol, an outward and visible sign of the inward reality—that the Phoenix, more than any other woman in the clan, represented the eternal flame.

As small children, Breanna and I had crushed ash into powder, brushed it over our roots, and danced through our tent in our clumsy, childlike way. Pretending to be the

163

Phoenix. I'd cried for joy the day they painted Breanna's hair.

And now it was my turn. After this, I really would be the Phoenix.

Deirdre shooed Shayla and me out of the practice tent. "Off with you now. Go to your dressing tables. Colleen will be there in a few minutes. Since there are two of you, I'm having Breanna help her."

I didn't need to be asked twice. I darted into the open sunlight and sprinted toward the practice tent. No reason for me to walk alongside Shayla and force both of us to pretend to be civil.

Especially when I had to summon a flash of anger at her every time I wanted to enter the magecraft labyrinth.

It wasn't supposed to be that way. We were supposed to practice magecraft with a calm, peaceful mind. Like Nolan told me to. But some part of me suspected that, even with focused practice, I wouldn't be able to replicate this new ability that so augmented my power if I focused on *peace*. I had to channel stronger emotions.

Even if using my anger was dangerous, I needed it to pass the mage test in time. Nolan had been practicing his whole life. I'd gotten magecraft in bits and pieces, a month or two at a time, for only a few years.

My jaw tightened as I ducked through the flap into the dressing tent. I *needed* those darker emotions.

I could only hope that they wouldn't destroy me.

Sweet, grandmotherly Colleen, who had been the Phoenix when my own mama was a child, was already waiting in the tent. A twinkle shone in her eyes. "Kyla," she said warmly, moving forward to hug me. "I'm so very proud of you."

When she released me, I stepped back and scuffed the ground with my foot. "Thanks, Colleen," I said. I wasn't shy by nature, but something about Colleen's unconditional warmth always made me feel small inside. As if I didn't measure up to her. I wished I could be half as compassionate and giving as she was.

The tent canvas rustled, and Shayla came in behind me.

"Shayla!" Colleen cried, rushing to embrace her.

Colleen even liked *Shayla*. Colleen *did* like everyone.

I gave a quiet little huff.

"Now," Colleen called. "Sit down at your dressing tables, each of you. We'll darken your roots first, and then weave the color in through the rest of your hair. Breanna will be here in a few minutes. She went down to Terra Market for amber dye. We only had enough for one dancer!" She chuckled. "Didn't expect I'd get to be doing hair for you both."

I spared a sideways glance at Shayla out of the corner of my eye, but Colleen didn't seem to notice.

"Go!" She waved her hands. "Sit!"

Suppressing a little chuckle, I moved to obey, flouncing toward my own vanity without another glance at Shayla. I sank onto the stool, and a mound of heavy fabric smacked me from behind. I whirled around just in time to see Colleen toss a large black robe at Shayla. "Put these on over your clothes, girls. Keeps the paint off them."

My robe had slumped to the floor, and I picked it up and shook it off. It was large, with oversized sleeves and buttons that ran all the way down the front. I shrugged into it, my fingers finding each tiny buttonhole. I'd just finished the last button when I heard Breanna's voice.

"I was lucky to find any amber paint at all!" she cried. "Think I might have found the last jar of it in the whole market."

"That'll do," called Colleen in her usual cheery voice. "I've mixed the dark brown here. Let me show you how to paint Kyla's hair."

They walked over, their loose skirts rustling. Breanna looked more relaxed than I'd seen her in weeks.

Colleen lifted a chunk of my hair. "Now, Breanna," she

said. "You'll want to paint piece by piece, making sure that the dye touches every strand of hair, top and bottom. I'll do the roots on both girls because it's hard to cover any mistakes made with the dark dye. But I'll have you do the other colors on Kyla, since those don't have to be as precise."

Colleen set a plate on the vanity table in front of me, and I took in the strong-smelling dye. A paintbrush rested atop the plate. Then Colleen grabbed a comb and ran it through my hair until every strand gleamed. "You ready?" she asked with a grin.

"Aye, ma'am!" I responded. Maybe too eagerly.

She dipped the end of the paintbrush into the dye and reached for a lock of my hair. I sucked in a breath. This was it. The transformation that would make it apparent to all that I was the Phoenix.

The dye felt cold when Colleen brushed it against my scalp. And the whole process took much longer than I expected. Colleen worked carefully with each piece of hair, conversing with Breanna in low tones. When she finished, she squeezed my shoulders. "We're going to go do the same thing on Shayla's hair, and then we'll take you both down to the creek to rinse out the dye. Once your hair is dry, we'll add in the colors."

I could see why Deirdre had given us the whole day off practice.

Hours later—after two separate dips in the too-cold creek—Breanna stood behind me, ruffling my hair with a cloth. "There you go," she said with a smile. "Brush it out and let it dry."

I stared at my reflection in the mirror, trying to find the Phoenix in the contours of my face or the confidence in my eyes. Because I couldn't see it yet in my hair—not while it was still dark with water. My stomach burned with anticipation.

"Let's go out in the sun," suggested Breanna. "Dry it off faster. The market?"

I nodded eagerly. I needed something to take my mind off the slow pace of drying hair, off my new appearance, off my roiling turmoil about the future.

Maybe I'd find a snail roll.

Breanna and I eased our way into the bustling market. The energy of the crowd buzzed around me, crackling like fire. "Let's go through the barn," Breanna said. "I want to buy some soap from Gerta, and her table is usually inside."

My fingers drifted up to brush against my still-damp hair, and I nodded. As we pushed our way down the crowded thoroughfare, I searched for the earth wizards I'd talked to last time I'd visited the market. But they were nowhere to be seen. No wares for sale today, perhaps.

Or maybe Jouko had gotten word of their murmurings and revoked their rent agreement. The thought made me feel sick. How would they feed their little ones then? Could they hope to find work—or at least land to rent—from one of the other powerful families in the area?

My thoughts were running away with me. Sellers often missed a day in the market. There was no reason for me to be alarmed.

The barn loomed in front of us, imposing with its massive cedarwood beams and carved doors. It had once belonged to a wealthy earth wizard with an affinity for racehorses. But since before I was born, it had been part of the Orivesi Terra Market, as shaded space for the vendors and customers.

We ducked inside, and I blinked against the sudden dimness. The air felt thick, the smells of sweat and cedar and fresh flowers blending together into an aroma that was equal parts intriguing and off-putting.

Merchants were set up in the old horse stalls, but they didn't aggressively hawk their wares at us as those outside did. No, these spaces went to the more prominent, established merchants. Those with enough money to pay for the privilege of selling inside rather than out in the baking sun.

Breanna and I lingered, floating from stall to stall, looking at the fabric and fruit and flowers.

"Are you ready for your last show?" I asked as we lingered over a few bright red apples. Breanna's final dance was tomorrow, and the thought curled in my stomach like sour sheep milk.

Breanna didn't visibly react. "I think so," she said, her voice steady. "I think it'd be harder if I weren't handing the role off to my little sister."

I pursed my lips. *And our bratty cousin.*

"Or if I had a husband I didn't love," she continued. "Darick has been so sweet. New wildflowers in the kitchen every day." She gave a little laugh, and I couldn't suppress a smile.

"I'm glad you didn't marry Gainor," I said.

Breanna snorted.

"Now that wasn't very ladylike." I smacked her on the arm. "You know, you've got to represent the Fintan as the Phoenix for another whole day. Can't have you making strange noises at the market."

She rolled her eyes and elbowed me in the side. "Impudent child. Maybe I'll just dance through my whole pregnancy and not let you be Phoenix after all. Wait to retire until after Mama marries *you* off to Gainor."

I groaned. "At least that one's already taken."

Breanna made a face. Gainor had married a woman three years older than me. His new wife was younger than his oldest daughter, and we'd all been properly horrified.

We browsed through the stalls a little longer, until we finally came to Gerta's table full of soaps. Breanna picked up soap after soap, smelling each one, and asking Gerta questions about which scents were best for pregnancy nausea. When she made her selections, she handed Gerta a few coins, and we made our way to the next stall.

After we finished our stroll through the barn, we walked out of the humid dankness and into the clear, warm sunshine. I gave a little sigh of contentment.

"One more stop," said Breanna.

I nodded, happy to let her do her shopping. I trailed behind her as she meandered down the central thoroughfare to a table covered in knickknacks. She walked straight to a silver-handled mirror and picked it up. "Your hair is dry," she said.

My heart pounded in my chest. The moment was here. When I'd really see myself, for the first time, as the Phoenix. I bit my lip and stepped toward Breanna, nodding eagerly.

Breanna turned the mirror around, and I took in my reflection. I couldn't suppress the smile that suffused my face. My roots, dark like a burnt-out ember. The colors of the eternal flame woven through my hair. So different than my usual single shade of red. I looked older. Sophisticated. Successful.

I looked like the Phoenix.

TWENTY-SIX

The first strains of music wafted through the air. The musicians would play the theme through three times before the actual dance began.

This was the last time the troupe would perform this routine. The last time Breanna would dance with the troupe at all. A gaping chasm had opened up in my stomach, and it felt hard to draw breath.

Shayla and I weren't performing tonight—not with our hair already dyed to signify that we were the Phoenixes. Two younger girls had been moved up from the understudy troupe to dance in our place.

"How are you feeling?" I asked Breanna as we left the dressing tent and began the walk to the stage.

Our last walk to the stage together.

She took a deep breath. "It's been a beautiful two years," she said. "I wouldn't trade that time for anything. But I think the next two years will be beautiful too."

Tears brimmed in my eyes, but I blinked them back. Breanna needed me to be strong for her tonight.

We approached the stage and stopped, looking out over the gathering audience. "Big crowd tonight," I said.

"Yes." A little smile turned up the corners of her lips. "It's going to be a show worth remembering."

"Your performances are always worth remembering." I looped my arm through hers and leaned my head against her shoulder. "I'm glad I get to watch from the audience tonight."

When we reached the bottom of the stairs, I wrapped my arms around her and gave her a quick peck on the cheek. "Fintan fire," I said.

"Fintan fire," she replied, reaching out and squeezing my hands.

And then she turned, ran up the stairs, and vanished behind the curtain. I took a long, shuddering breath and turned to find a seat. Scanning the crowd, I found an empty chair next to Liam, who sat at the end of the row.

I pushed my way toward him. "Mind if I join you?" I asked.

"By all means," he said, gesturing toward the empty seat.

I narrowed my gaze. "Shouldn't you be doing something . . . mage-ish?"

He shook his head. "Not on my day off, I shouldn't. I am going to sit here and watch the dance and then whisk Aislinn off through the festival, like we're just attendees." He grinned. "Sweep her off her feet."

With a smile, I said, "Good." Then the mirth dropped away from my face. "Liam, has your mama said anything . . ."

He grimaced. "About how she's scheming with your mama? I'm afraid so."

"Just so we're clear, I never—"

He waved a hand in my face to stop me. "I know, I know. You and Nolan are meant to be. Don't worry. I know you're not in on our mamas' nonsense. My folks wanted us to go have dinner with your family about a month ago, but I put a stop to it."

Meant to be? My heart leaped at the idea, and then I wrinkled my nose. Why did everything have to be so complicated? If Nolan and I were meant to be . . . that meant I'd have to leave the clan. Unless I could somehow do the impossible and convince the council to let Nolan in. And as I sat there, looking at the beauty of the festival, the idea of leaving the Fintan made my chest ache.

"Good," I said, turning back to Liam. "Just wanted to make sure there wasn't any awkwardness between us. I value your friendship and Aislinn's."

The music changed in tempo, and a hush fell over the crowd. "Shhh," Liam whispered. "Aislinn's about to come onstage."

It had been almost a year since I'd watched the troupe perform, and even though I knew the dances by heart, I found myself enraptured in the show. But it was Breanna's performance that brought me to tears. Her technique, her artistry, the raw emotion she brought to her dancing. She was perfect.

What a legacy to live up to.

When she struck her final pose, I shot to my feet, clapping wildly. The crowd wasn't far behind, rising one by one from their seats to give Breanna a standing ovation.

Fireworks boomed in the sky, a dazzling light show in honor of Breanna's final performance. A flash of bright yellow hurtled into the air and then exploded in a wreath of white and blue. The sparks showered down toward the stage, but faded into nothing before they reached the ground. Another explosion, and this time the fireworks shone in shades of purple and red. Three quick booms in succession, and a million points of yellow-white light hovered in the sky for a fraction of a moment like a curtain of stars. Then they fell and blinked out of existence.

Even from my place fifteen rows back, I could see that Breanna was crying. When she vanished behind the curtain, I darted out of my seat and up the steps, the fireworks still exploding in the sky. Swishing through the curtain, I found the troupe dancers huddled around Breanna. Aislinn glanced over and saw me and welcomed me into the mass of hugs.

When we broke apart, Breanna's eyeliner was smeared.

"Thank you all," she said, her voice quavering. "This has been the privilege of a lifetime."

Breanna assured me that she was fine but exhausted, that she hadn't slept well the night before and wanted nothing more than to go to bed early and deal with her emotions tomorrow.

I went to bed early, too, but lay awake, tossing and turning, unable to force myself to sleep. My feelings were too big and overwhelming—grief, excitement, trepidation. Tomorrow night I'd dance my first show as Phoenix.

The faint light outside the tent went dark. The nightwatch were extinguishing the torches, marking midnight. With a sigh, I sat up and reached for my small pouch, in which I carried the coal that Nolan had given me and the strange white marble of the labyrinth. Perhaps just holding their familiar smoothness would ground me, help me calm my turbulent feelings. But my pouch wasn't among the crumpled clothes lying on the ground.

I knitted my eyebrows and groped through another pile of clothes. Then another.

It wasn't there.

The realization hit me at once. I'd left it on Breanna's vanity in the dressing tent before the show and hadn't returned to pick it up.

At least it gave me something to do. I changed into proper clothes and then slipped out of my room and out of the tent, trying to rustle the canvas as little as possible so I wouldn't wake Mama and Papa. With only the light of the moon, the stars, and a handful of phoenixflies, I wended my way through the tents and out toward the festival grounds. In the darkness, the great tents, the stage, the torches all looked eerie. Almost dead. I walked a little faster.

When I neared the dressing tent, I stopped and cocked my head. Was there . . . someone crying in the dressing tent?

Breanna, I thought. *She couldn't sleep either and came back here so she wouldn't wake Darick with her tears.*

I pushed through the tent flap to go to my sister and comfort her.

But it wasn't Breanna. Instead, Shayla sat at her mirrored vanity, her face buried in her arms, sobs wracking her body.

I swallowed and took a step back. Awkwardness churned in my stomach. I needed to slip out of here like a phantom and pretend I'd never come. That I hadn't caught Shayla crying.

But then Shayla looked up and saw me. A sob caught in her throat.

"What are you doing here?" she demanded.

"I . . . forgot something," I said, stepping forward and striding as quickly as I could toward Breanna's vanity. "I'll just get it and be on my way. Sorry to bother you."

I grabbed the pouch and tied it around my waist. Then I walked back to the tent flap . . . and stopped. Turned back toward Shayla. I didn't even know why.

"Is something wrong?" I asked, my voice gentle.

Shayla shook her head fiercely. "Go away."

"I'm sorry," I said. Hesitated. "Is it about the whole Phoenix thing?"

She bit down on her lip and curled her hands into fists. "I told you to leave me alone."

"Fine," I snapped. "You haven't wanted to talk to me in years. Why would now be any different?"

She regarded me with an icy stare. "*I* haven't wanted to talk to *you?*"

I almost laughed. "You wouldn't even speak to me at the wake after Grandmama passed away."

Now fire blazed in her eyes. "Of course I didn't. Why would I waste time chasing someone who couldn't be bothered to make time for me? At some point, I cut my losses."

I blinked, once, twice, three times. "What are you talking about?"

Shayla's jaw tightened. "After Mama died. She . . . was everything. My world. You *knew* that."

The realization crept over me like tendrils, the shame wrapping around my throat. Shayla didn't have any other brothers and sisters. Her papa was affectionate enough but . . . busy. Always busy.

And Shayla's mama had doted on her. She'd died when we were eleven, the day we arrived in Orivesi for a month of shows.

I'd spent the whole month running around with Nolan.

So that's what Shayla never forgave me for.

Shayla wiped at her eyes. "Go!" she bellowed.

I took a hesitant step toward her. "I'm sorry," I said. "I was selfish. I didn't realize—"

"Go!" she yelled again, slamming her hand on the vanity.

I backed through the tent flap and ran into the night.

The next evening, I found myself behind the curtain, dressed in full Phoenix regalia, my fingers itching to touch my perfect hair. I looked every inch the Phoenix. Shayla was sick tonight—or that's what she'd said—and Deirdre and I had hurried to modify the show so that I could dance alone. So here I was, waiting to go onstage as principal dancer of the Fintan for the first time.

I hoped I'd make Papa proud. Nolan wasn't out there tonight—there'd been an emergency with one of the sheep at the farm—but he'd see me dance soon enough.

From where I stood, I could hear the murmurs of the gathering crowd. I swallowed. I wasn't nervous. Not exactly. I'd worked hard, and I knew the dance. And I was no stranger to the stage.

But still, my heart felt . . . disturbed. I searched my mind and tried to parse out what I was feeling.

Sadness. For Shayla. For Breanna. For myself.

I glanced around the edge of the curtain, my eyes searching for Breanna. Couldn't find her in the crowd.

And then I heard her voice behind me. "Hey," she said.

I turned around, the emotion swelling thick in my throat, and pulled her into a fierce hug.

"Hey, what's wrong?" she whispered in my ear. "Are you nervous?"

If I'd been able to utter any words, I might have said, *I'm so sorry that it's not you dancing tonight,* or *you were the greatest fire dancer the troupe has ever seen.*

When I pulled back, tears brimmed in Breanna's eyes. "You'll do wonderfully," she said.

I still couldn't speak.

"I know," she murmured. "I know." Her right hand rested on her midsection. "But it's okay."

Everything in me wanted to ask her how any of this could be okay—how she could accept that she was done dancing. But the first strains of the music wafted across the stage. It was my moment.

"Go," she said. "I'll be cheering you on."

I took a deep breath, accepted a lit fire wand from a solemn-faced mage, and moved back to my spot behind the curtains. The music hit my first beat, and I leaped out, flying into a jeté.

I was glad that this dance—The Silver Swan—was a tragedy. I gave my emotions full rein as I flowed through the movements, barely noticing when the troupe came out to dance behind me. Every moment of this dance was for Breanna.

At the final pose of the first act, I threw the baton up, watching it arc in the air. When I caught it and whipped it forward, I shot a shower of sparks out of the wand, just as I had on a similar move in Scarlet Moon.

The crowd gasped and then broke into applause. I maintained the forlorn, tragic expression appropriate to the dance, but when I disappeared behind the curtain, a huge smile spread across my face.

I had about a minute to breathe while the troupe danced before I needed to go back on. My gaze flickered across the room. Breanna wasn't here anymore. She must have gone down into the audience to watch the dance with everyone else. With everyone who wasn't a fire dancer.

She'd moved on into the next stage of her life. And though there was searing pain and a sense of loss, I hoped with all my heart that she would find nothing but happiness in the days ahead.

TWENTY-SEVEN

"You did marvelously." Papa hugged me to his side when I reached the grass after the show. Tears brimmed in his eyes. A phoenixfly fluttered past his face, bright against the night, shedding blue and purple sparks. My heart soared. Everything about this evening was perfect. Except that Nolan wasn't here.

"My darling daughter!" Mama cried, bowling into us. "You were as lovely as Breanna. Oh, my dear. My girls are the two best dancers in the history of the festival."

The festivalgoers were looking at us, but I didn't care. Warmth bubbled up in my chest. Even Mama was proud of me.

She leaned over and whispered, "Caolinn and I would like to announce something big for you and Liam soon."

Heat flooded my cheeks. I jerked back. "What are you talking about?" I hissed, glancing around to make sure Mama hadn't been overheard.

Blazes, Mama would probably be *overheard* on purpose so she could start the rumors that Liam and I would soon be betrothed.

A hurt expression overtook her face. "You know very well what I'm talking about, young lady."

"I haven't passed my seventeenth birthday yet." I crossed my arms. "What would you even announce?"

She sulked. "Well, it wouldn't be *official* yet. But we should take advantage of your triumph tonight, Kyla. You'll never be as valuable on the marriage market as you are right now."

I wanted to be angry. I waited, gritting my teeth, for the rage to well in my chest. For the heated words to come spilling out at Mama. But they didn't.

Because I wasn't angry.

I was hurt.

You'll never be as valuable on the marriage market as you are right now.

Valuable?

"Come, now." Papa put an arm around Mama's shoulders. "Let's go home. Kyla's had a big day. We'll discuss this another time." He kissed Mama's head and pulled her away, then turned around and shot me a wink.

At least Papa was on my side.

But Mama's words burned in my mind. I kept turning them over and over again. *You'll never be as valuable on the marriage market as you are right now.*

Was that how Mama thought of me? As a commodity on the *marriage market*? I knew she was eager to get her daughters settled, but . . .

My gaze followed a bright red phoenixfly as it fluttered past me and landed squarely in the middle of a flaming blue torch. Any other insect would disintegrate in the fire. But a moment later, the phoenixfly emerged from the blaze, its wings now flaming blue.

Hadn't Mama just seen me dance? Hadn't she just called me one of the best dancers in the history of the festival?

Not that I believed her words to be objective. A mother was allowed to be partial. But how could she say such a thing and then turn around and try to have me married off the moment it was lawful?

She knew that I wanted more than what a marriage to Liam would give me. She *knew*.

On this point I'd been clear: I didn't want to marry young. Not before I'd satisfied my ambitions, accomplished everything I'd set out to do.

And I wasn't done yet. Not nearly.

Sucking in a deep breath, I set out at a jog for the dressing tent. I needed to get out of my costume. And then spend an hour or two practicing magecraft to burn away all my angst.

I set four bushes on fire that night. While I managed to tamp the blazes out quickly enough, I winced at the ash-laden ruins each fire had left in its wake.

Even if there *wasn't* an arsonist running around these parts, the evidence I left behind after magecraft practice might be enough to alarm the council.

I just couldn't consistently get it under control.

With a sigh, I rubbed my temples with soot-tinted fingers and then walked back in the direction of camp.

My sandaled feet scuffed in the grass, and I tilted my head back to look at the stars as I walked. My eyes traced the phoenixbird constellation, and I sucked in a deep breath of clear, cool air.

I was almost to my tent, now, and I wiped my hands on my skirt and hoped Mama and Papa were asleep already so they wouldn't see my sweaty, disheveled state.

"Kyla?"

Breanna sat outside my tent, her face serene.

"Everything alright?" I asked.

"Just waiting for you," she said. "Papa told me about your fight with Mama."

"Calling it a *fight* is an overstatement," I muttered. "Papa pulled her out of there before it got ugly."

Breanna chuckled. "That's for the best. Wouldn't do to have the Phoenix fighting at the festival. The council would pitch a fit."

I gave her a wan smile. "It would have been memorable."

She clambered to her feet, one hand resting on her stomach. "Take a walk with me."

I slipped my arm through hers, and we wandered amid the tents and back toward the festival grounds.

"You were beautiful tonight," Breanna said. "I was so proud to be your sister."

"I'm always proud to be your sister," I quipped.

She laughed and punched me in the arm. "You know what I mean."

We reached the outer edge of the festival grounds, which lay dark and quiet after a long night of revelry. I swallowed. The torches were out. Breanna had waited up late for me to return.

"I'm sorry to keep you up."

She waved her hand. "I'm not going anywhere tomorrow. Wouldn't have been able to sleep, anyway. There's been so much on my mind."

"Are you okay?" I asked. "Was it as hard as you expected? To give it up?"

We reached the outermost table, and she slid onto the bench. I sat next to her.

"Nay," she said at last. "I felt the baby move today."

I squealed and whirled toward her, then reached a tentative hand toward her stomach. "May I?"

She rolled up her blouse so that I could press a hand to her bare skin. I rested my palm there, holding my breath, waiting.

The baby didn't move.

After a minute, I scowled at Breanna's pregnant belly. "Not much of a performer, are you, little one?"

Breanna laughed, and her face was free of all the grief and anger that had burdened her recently. I leaned back and studied her.

"You're different, somehow," I said. "Is it motherhood? Are you . . ." I didn't know how to finish.

Her smile grew thoughtful. "I don't think so. At least not in the way everyone says. I felt the baby move today, and it was wonderful, of course. It did remind me of all the happy things to come. But . . . it's more than that."

I looked at her expectantly.

"Darick made a cradle for the baby, and he showed it to me today. I can't wait for you to see it. It's beautiful. And he was so excited to show it to me. He'd made it with so much love."

I waited, sensing there was more.

"He brought it in when I was just about to make bread. And when he left, I decided to make an extra loaf to bring to Saiorse."

I nodded and leaned against Breanna's shoulder.

"Saoirse has been so sad since her husband's passing, you know? But she brightened so much when I brought her that loaf of bread. It was the first smile I've seen from her in months. And it made me realize something. The secret to dancing that I forgot to teach you."

"Wait, what?" I retraced the contours of Breanna's words. "This is about dancing?"

"It's about everything," she said, gazing up at the sky.

Had the pregnancy made her brainsick? "You're going to have to explain this one."

She looked over at me. "Why did you dance so well tonight?"

My mouth twisted. "Because . . . I worked hard?"

She shook her head. "More than that. You're always a lovely dancer. You execute the steps with such strength. You carry yourself with grace. You add magical flourishes that will definitely get you in trouble someday."

I chuckled.

"But tonight, it was like your feet barely touched the ground. Why?"

The answer came to me in a moment. "Because I was dancing for you."

"Love." Her eyes sparkled. "I always performed my best when I danced out of love. For Darick. Or you. Or Deirdre. Or anyone, really, as long as I was able to channel that love."

My nose wrinkled. "I'm not sure feeling *love* for Deirdre will help me dance better."

She elbowed me. "She's not so bad once you get to know her."

"I'll take your word for it," I muttered.

Breanna's face softened. "Deirdre has . . . had a hard life. She doesn't talk about it. Not really. But bits and pieces of her story have come out over the years. I have sympathy for her."

"Even if she's a terrifying troll?"

Breanna knocked me off the bench with her shoulder, and I collapsed to the ground, laughing.

Then Breanna gasped. "Kyla! Quick! Baby's moving!"

I darted upward, my hand outstretched, and Breanna pressed it to her belly. Sure enough, beneath my fingers, I felt a rippling sensation.

A grin spread across my face, and I lifted my eyes to meet Breanna's. Love.

Another wave pulsed in her belly, and after a moment, I dropped my hand. "I think it's a girl," I said. "And someday, her dancing will put yours and mine to shame."

TWENTY-EIGHT

The next morning, I dragged myself to practice bleary-eyed and exhausted.

"Kyla Brannon!" Deirdre snapped her fingers at me as I stumbled into the tent. "What is the meaning of this? Are you ill? Drunk?" Her tone reached a frantic pitch.

I ran a hand through my hair. "Nay, ma'am. Just tired. Didn't sleep well last night."

"Well." Deidre's voice softened, and she reached down to smooth her flowing skirt. "That's understandable. The first time on a brand-new stage always feels like magic."

I tilted my head, studying her. A soft smile played at the edges of her mouth and then vanished.

Huh. Deirdre had been the Phoenix years ago. I'd known that. But I'd always thought of her as our teacher, not as an actual dancer. Breanna's words from the night before played in my mind. What kind of tragic story did Deirdre keep buried beneath that stern exterior?

It wouldn't hurt me to be a bit nicer to Deirdre.

"Aye. It did feel like magic." No need to tell Deirdre that I was being quite literal. "I . . . just had to walk around for a long time afterward."

"Well, don't make a habit of it," she said. "We need you fresh at practice."

"Of course, ma'am."

I didn't know what else to say, so I glanced at the sea of dancers for help, but no one was paying me any attention.

Except for Shayla, who had her arms crossed and was glowering at me.

The shame threatened to curl around my heart again, and I couldn't face it. So I grasped at something else. Anything else. Frustration tingled in my chest instead. That was better. More bearable.

Why was she always like this? I was well and truly over it. *I'm sorry I was selfish when we were eleven.* Bitterness laced my thoughts. *But we were children. It was a long time ago. For blazes' sake, can't we move on?*

Deirdre clapped. "Places, everyone!"

I darted to the wall to grab the baton for the first dance and hurried to my spot. No time to worry about Shayla today. I barely had the energy to dance.

Love, I thought, remembering the feeling of Breanna's baby—my niece, I felt sure—moving inside her.

How could I dance with love? What did that even mean? I'd done it the night before, right after an emotional moment with Breanna. But how could I make a choice to summon *love* every time I danced?

It was all still confusing. But I would try. For Breanna. And for her baby.

And so, for the next several hours, I pointed my toes, leaped into the air, and tossed fire props high above my head, all while trying to summon the emotion of love. Some of my jumps and spins were better than others, but frustration grew in my chest with every move I executed. I was dancing well—dancing adequately, for the Phoenix—but I wasn't finding the poetic fluidity that had come so naturally to me the evening before, on the stage.

And worse, Shayla was doing better than I was.

I stopped midway through a spin and crouched down, trying to dig deep into my consciousness, to figure out what I was missing. In the corner of my mind, a white door beckoned me, inviting me inside the all-white maze where I stored my fire magic. But I shook it away.

Not there. Not right now.

Instead, I guided myself toward the memories of last night's dance.

"Kyla?" Deirdre's voice intruded on my concentration, but I raised a hand and waved her away.

"Just a second," I said, my voice distant. "I almost have it."

Deirdre harrumphed, but I brushed it away. I'd deal with her wrath in a second. I just had to remember . . .

The cheers of the crowd. The energy tingling in the air. The gleam in Breanna's eyes as she wished me well. The overpowering love I felt for her, for the child she carried inside her. The feel of the baby moving beneath my fingers. I let the feeling overtake me again, rushing through me in waves.

My eyes snapped open, and I stood up as straight as a cedar tree. "I've got it," I said.

Deirdre arched one elegant eyebrow and then shook her head. "Whatever you say," she muttered. Then she called out, "Everyone, let's start the piece again. Places!"

When I turned to take my place, I ignored Shayla's glare. I couldn't focus on her. Not if I wanted to keep ahold of this love I'd found within myself. So I looked past her and took my first position. Deirdre clapped her hands and called, "Five, six, seven, eight."

Pirouette. Step right. Glide. Baton up.

I threw the wand into a perfect arc. It sliced through the air, and I caught it just as I moved into my first jump.

For Breanna. And her baby.

With every step, I channeled the love I felt for my sister and for my niece. I thought again of the life I wanted for the baby, how I hoped she would have choices I'd never been given. How desperately I wanted her future to be beautiful.

In the back of my mind, an insistent thought buzzed— that she wouldn't have any more options than I did if no one forced the council to give her those options—but I set it aside to consider later. For now, I needed to dance.

And dance I did. I flew through the steps, executing each one to perfection, exuding grace and strength and vulnerability, even while dancing across from Shayla. The buzz swelled to a crescendo in my mind. Breanna was right. Love, somehow, gave me wings.

I hit the last pose with closed eyes, and the room went silent. When I dared open them, Deirdre was staring at me.

She sniffed. "Well, Miss Brannon, your methods of preparation are rather unorthodox, but I'm quite pleased with the results. That was the best you've ever danced. Perhaps excepting last night."

Someone started clapping behind me, and when I turned around, I realized it was Aislinn. She was grinning at me, and I shook my head to try to get her to stop. But one by one, the other dancers joined in, until everyone was applauding.

Well, everyone except Shayla. She was standing there with her lips quirked to the side and a withering glare on her face. Then she hurried over to Deirdre and whispered something in her ear. Deidre nodded at her, and Shayla disappeared through the tent flap.

Good riddance.

The applause died down, and Aislinn said, "What happened, Kyla? I've never seen you dance like that. It was like you were . . . floating or something."

"I've never seen anyone dance like that," murmured Ciara.

I opened my mouth and then closed it again. The tent fabric rustled in the breeze. How could I explain to them what had happened? It had been such a sacred, intimate moment, and I couldn't find words that wouldn't make it sound . . . silly. Laughable.

"I . . . I don't know," I said. How could I hold those moments up for mockery? I vowed to tell them. Someday. When

I had better words to explain it, when they wouldn't dismiss what I was saying as stargazing rubbish. "I'll let you know when I've figured it out."

But Deirdre was wading into the crowd of dancers, waving her arms to recapture everyone's attention. "Stop heaping praise on Kyla, or it'll go to her head," she snapped. "Kyla has worked hard for this, and her reward is that she dances beautifully. Put in the work, and you'll dance beautifully too."

Aislinn's eyes narrowed, and I knew she didn't believe Deirdre's explanation. Everyone in this troupe worked hard. Some of them had worked just as hard as me—or harder. Despite the skeptical look Aislinn was giving me, I knew I couldn't contradict Deirdre. At least not publicly.

She might tolerate my long, eccentric, crouched pause, but she'd have my head for defiance. And Shayla would be only too happy to step over my dead body to claim the entire role as her own.

TWENTY-NINE

Despite the hours of dancing, I didn't feel tired when practice ended. I felt exhilarated. I changed into my loose-fitting clothes and then fairly flew down to the river, where Nolan was waiting for me under our favorite willow tree.

"Hey." A grin tugged at his lips when he saw my smile. "Good day?"

"The best," I said. Then my forehead crinkled. "I . . . I've been thinking a lot about Breanna's baby."

He tilted his head. "Oh?"

A flush suffused my face. He hadn't thought I meant I was thinking a lot about babies, generally, had he? I plunged ahead, desperate to rid the situation of any tinge of awkwardness. "I want her to have options. I mean, I know that it might be a boy, but . . . I don't think she is." Tears brimmed in my eyes. "I think I'm going to have a little niece, Nolan."

He reached out, grabbed my hand, and pulled me down to sit beside him on the boulder. "That will be wonderful," he said softly.

You don't understand. "I don't want her to grow up like I did," I muttered, swiping at my tears. "I don't want her to grow up feeling like she *has* to be a dancer in order to distinguish herself. Becoming the Phoenix was always . . . my only option at ambition, you know? I mean, I love dancing. I really do. But what if it wasn't really what I wanted *most* all along?"

He threaded his fingers through mine and squeezed my hand. "I know, Kyla. I know."

I sucked in a deep breath, letting the music of birdsong, the dance of the green light streaming through the treetops, and the soft smell of honeysuckle in the air steady my nerves and slow my thoughts. "But why should only one girl at a time get to succeed?" I asked. "Why should it be such an unusual circumstance for Shayla and I both to be crowned? Why must all the others be disappointed, even if they're smart and skilled and talented and hardworking?"

"It's not a fair system. That's part of why you want to be a mage." With his free hand, he picked at a patch of moss spreading across the rock.

Something sour and choking rose up in my throat, and I shook my head. "I *do* want to be a mage. It's not fair that I can't be. But . . . it can't just be about me."

"Hmm?"

I sat up straighter and held his gaze, hoping that the intensity burning in my core shone clearly in my eyes. "We have to break the system," I said. "The council can't just make an exception for me. We have to change the clan so that every girl who comes after me has a world full of options."

Nolan chuckled. "No one ever accused you of not being ambitious enough."

A dragonfly shot past me in pursuit of a smaller bug, and I flinched away from it on instinct. But it disappeared into the trees. It was no doubt far more interested in acquiring its dinner than it was in scorching me with a tiny spark of fire shot from its mouth.

Even the Fintan didn't like dragonflies.

I turned back to Nolan and held my chin high. "Do you think I can't do it?"

He ran a hand through his blond hair. "I think you're young and female in a society that values old men. I'm not saying you *can't* do it; I'm just saying it's going to be hard to get them to listen to you."

I chewed my lip. "They value men, yes, but young men are often thane. The youngest thane in history was fourteen."

He waved his hand. "I know the story. And yes, the thane is sometimes young, but most of the council is a spry eighty-two years of age."

I tried to suppress a laugh, but it came out as a snort. "They're not that old."

I thought of Desmond and Rory, who had been on the council since Mama was a girl—and then added, "Well, most of them."

"Like I was saying." He stood up and brushed the dirt off his pants. "They're not likely to be enthusiastic about change. I mean, think of all the stories—it's young people who lead the charge to make change happen."

I leaped to my feet. "Don't you see?" I began to pace back and forth across the clearing. "That's what I've been saying. We have to *make* it happen."

He crossed his arms. "You keep saying *we*, but I'm not even Fintan."

I stopped beside him and rested a hand on his shoulder. "You will be," I said. "Because that's one of the changes we have to see through."

A sigh wracked his chest, and then he said, "Okay. Just tell me when you have a plan."

Frustration coursed through my body—because I *still* didn't know how we were going to do any of this. "You could challenge for thaneship at the torch ceremony," I said weakly.

Nolan laughed aloud. "They'd arrest me."

"I know, I know," I grumbled. "And only mages can challenge, so they'd declare you disqualified even if you beat my uncle in mage combat."

"*You* could challenge," he said. "If you've convinced them to make you a mage by then."

This time I laughed at Nolan. "That would go over even better, wouldn't it?"

His eyes sparkled. "I'm sure they'd be delighted to watch you spar with your uncle."

"Pretty sure they'd arrest me."

"Probably."

"Arrest you for what?" asked a familiar too-sweet voice.

Blazes. I turned toward the voice and took in Shayla. Her Phoenix hair was tied back with a cord, and she tossed it over her shoulder. The expression on her face was entirely too self-satisfied for my comfort.

"What are you doing here?" I asked, trying to keep my frustration under control.

"Getting what I want," she said breezily.

"To fall and trip in the mud?" I retorted.

She rolled her eyes. "Simple girl. No wonder you couldn't win outright, even after you cheated in the audition."

"I'm sure I don't know what—"

The thane and two of the younger council members stepped into the glade behind Shayla. I stiffened. What had Shayla told them?

Nolan shuffled back a step.

"Well," said the thane. "Shayla was right on one count. Kyla, would you care to tell me what my niece is doing consorting with the son of a defector?"

"He's a friend," I said, my voice tight.

"Shayla claims he's been teaching you magecraft. That you used it to get ahead at the audition. But that can't be true, can it?" His eyes narrowed on me.

I swallowed. Shayla was forcing my hand. If I lied now, the thane might drop the matter. But then I'd never be able to step forward and ask them to train me.

"I didn't cheat," I said firmly.

Out of the corner of my eye, Nolan scuffed his foot on the ground.

"A deft evasion of the question." The thane lifted his chin, as if daring me to try again. "Choose your words carefully, Kyla. Shayla brought me a note that she says you wrote to this boy." He pulled a small piece of parchment out of his pocket and held it out to me.

With wooden movements, I reached to take it. It was in my handwriting. I glanced at the note. A handful of phrases leaped out at me. *Meet me tomorrow . . . spend our time practicing . . . lost in the magic.*

This was a letter I'd written to Nolan, that I'd planned to hide in the oak in case he wasn't there to meet me. I'd put it in my pocket . . . a few days before Aislinn saw Shayla rummaging through my things.

My eyes burned as I looked up at Shayla. If I'd betrayed her five years ago, this betrayal was far worse. The little snake had held onto the letter, waiting for this moment to destroy me.

There was no denying the note. This was it, then. We had to plead our case even though we weren't ready, even though we had no plan.

Maybe this is what we should have done all along.

For strength, I reached into the pouch tied around my waist and ran my fingers over the two stones inside it: the coal that Nolan had given me, and the marble that had been a gift from the magic itself.

Swallowing, I glanced at Nolan. He returned my gaze and gave a small nod.

Turning back to the thane, I held my head high and matched his fierce expression. "I'd like to request an audience with the council."

THIRTY

Nolan and I stood in the council tent. Before us, in a semicircle, sat the twelve members of the Fintan High Council.

Old Rory peered at me quizzically. His voluminous eyebrows reminded me of a pair of squirrels. To his left, Cormac Flynn—Liam's papa—looked more sympathetic. Perhaps there was some hope. On the far end, Gainor Byrne just seemed bored, like he wanted to be home with his much-younger wife.

I sucked in a deep breath as my uncle took his seat in the middle. "Now," he said. "Tell us what this is all about, Kyla."

There were so many things I wanted to say. And I was sure that I wasn't going to say any of them eloquently. I could only speak from the heart and hope it would be enough.

"I come before you today to plead with you to consider two requests," I began, trying to choose each word as carefully as I could. "Fintan blood flows in my veins, just as it does in yours. The fire has fascinated me since I was a small child, calling to me as it did to each of you."

Niall Hannigan openly rolled his eyes.

I fixed my gaze on the torches behind them so I wouldn't lose my nerve. Another deep breath. "When I was small, I met Nolan Malone at the festival, when the Fintan were performing here in Orivesi. He knew a little magecraft and taught it to me."

The thane looked at Nolan. "And how did you know such a thing, outsider?" His voice was cold, his face stern.

Nolan swallowed. "My papa taught me. Just a little."

The council burst into frenzied conversation.

"Such a thing is forbidden," cried Old Rory.

Nolan raised his hands. "Let me speak," he called.

The council quieted, but the suspicion in their eyes had only deepened.

"You know my papa left the clan to marry my mama. Perhaps you also know that she died twelve years ago."

This seemed to come as news to about half of the council, but the others nodded stoically.

Nolan continued, "My older brother Brody . . ."

I tilted my head. An older brother named Brody?

Nolan didn't look at me as he spoke, his words coming faster and faster. "He was gifted. Unlike any child my papa had ever seen. But my papa believed the council. Believed it was too dangerous to teach anyone outside the confines of the clan. So he didn't. He just told Brody to control it. To tamp it down."

My hand flew to my mouth as the pieces came together in my mind.

Nolan continued, "The fire burned too hot in Brody. He figured out on his own how to light a spark. He was only seven. Didn't understand the danger. When Papa found out, he was angry. Shouted at him. Brody stormed off, yelling that he was going to learn magecraft and go live with the Fintan. He went into the barn. Mama followed him to try to comfort him. To talk sense into his head. She was carrying the baby with her. Papa walked down to the lake to clear his head."

A tear tracked down Nolan's cheek. Sensitive and kind though he was, I'd never seen him cry before. "In his anger, Brody set the barn on fire. When Papa saw the flames, he ran home as fast as he could to try to put it out, but it was too late. Brody, my mama, and the baby all died. Because Brody had figured out just enough magecraft to be danger-ous and didn't know how to treat it with proper respect. My papa decided that day that his children would learn enough magecraft to respect it."

The suspicion had faded from the councilors' faces. Well, most of them, anyway. Gainor Byrne seemed especially horrified, and tears brimmed in his eyes.

"Can you blame him?" Nolan choked out the last words. He stepped back.

I strongly suspected that the council did not blame Dallan Malone for his choice. But fear buzzed in the back of my head. The law was the law. Would they risk upsetting millennia of tradition for . . . anything?

Their attention returned to me. Time to speak again. Where had I left off? I was still awash in the horror of Nolan's story.

"Nolan knows enough to be a mage," I said. "And I do too. And so here are my requests: that you allow me to take the mage test and to become a mage if I pass." I wanted to ask that they let all girls take the mage test, but I decided to not push my luck. If I became a mage, I would use that position to work for the women of the clan. But it wasn't strategic to ask for everything at once. "And I would like the Malones to be given the choice of whether to rejoin the clan or not. Their mama is gone. The only ones remaining are of Fintan blood, and they all have the fire in their veins."

Dead silence.

Hope fluttered in my chest. Were they considering my words? It certainly seemed like Cormac, and maybe Gainor, were thinking hard.

Then Niall scoffed. "But you're a girl."

My uncle stood, a storm darkening his eyes. "I am empathetic to the plight of the Malones," he said. "Do not think me heartless."

My fragile hope shattered.

"But the choice to leave is final," he said. "We cannot water down our bloodline and slowly lose our magic. To do so would bring nothing but poverty and ruin for the clan. Dallan Malone made his choice. And Kyla, you must make yours."

Nothing to lose. "I choose to take the mage test."

He chuckled. One by one, the other council members caught his merriment. Niall Hannigan burst into uproarious laughter. Most of the others smirked at me. Even Cormac couldn't suppress a condescending smile.

My face warmed, and I could feel each thudding beat of my heart. They thought me a joke?

I raised my hands and sent out tendrils of energy toward the torches behind the council table. With a jerk of my hand, I extinguished them. Didn't even need to whisper the word.

The council members fell silent. Then my uncle said, "Kyla, I apologize for laugh—"

But I didn't want to hear his false apology. I closed my eyes, and the labyrinth was close at hand. I didn't need to think of my resentment toward Shayla. I had enough resentment and rage flowing in me to burn down the whole tent. But I suppressed it, controlled it enough to summon only a small orb of fire, letting it hover over my hand. I opened my eyes in the dim light of the tent. Sunlight still peeked through the canvas, showing me the faces of the council members, but only barely. I shaped the orb into a phoenixfly and sent it to flutter around the heads of the councilors. They shifted away from it, as if they were afraid it might explode into an inferno.

I called the fire back and kept it hovering over my hand. "I know too much magecraft," I said. "You can't afford not to train me. It's better to ensure I am fully trained in all the ways of a Fintan mage."

My uncle tilted his head. "All those fires here in Orivesi. Did you set them, trying to practice?"

My cheeks warmed, and I hoped the council couldn't see my blush in the dim light. Mind racing, I considered my options. Was it a test? Had the thane already figured out the truth? If I lied, would they think I'd been setting fires all through the county?

Swallowing, I said, "I was able to put them all out. All except one, the night I injured my ankle. I can ex—"

"Enough!" called my uncle. He snapped his fingers, and the torches flared to life again. "Kyla, I won't hear of this. And you will learn not to defy the council." His eyebrows knit together, as if he were considering his next words. And then his face relaxed. "For your defiance, you must suffer consequences. If such a breaking of the order is left unpunished, the community is harmed. For order cannot survive disorder. Kyla Brannon, you are no longer a fire dancer of the Fintan. You will not dance another festival show as long as you live."

I understood each of his words but couldn't string them together to fully comprehend their meaning. "What did you say?" I asked weakly.

"You are no longer the Phoenix," he replied, looking almost regretful. "You are no longer a fire dancer. You may choose whether you will stay in the clan and submit to the council or go with this boy and never return. But"—his face softened—"I will not force you to make that choice today." His gaze snapped to Nolan. "Leave," he hissed. "And I don't want to see you or your family in our encampment or at our festival ever again."

"You're making a mistake," said Nolan, his voice hoarse. He bowed his head, his jaw tight, and backed out of the tent. What else could he do? We were powerless against the will of the council.

Would Nolan want to be alone after this? Or would he meet me down at our usual place so we could discuss the blazing situation we'd found ourselves in?

Oh, how Shayla would be satisfied.

Then the realization hit me. The thane's words. Like a slap.

You are no longer the Phoenix. You are no longer a fire dancer.

"With all due respect," I said, each word strangled, like it was gasping for breath. "Uncle, you cannot take my place as Phoenix, as a fire dancer, away from me. The council has to agree. Unanimously." I trained my gaze, one by one, on the councilors who had seemed more sympathetic. Last of all, I cast pleading eyes on Cormac.

Old Rory stood. "I affirm," he said.

Niall Hannigan added his voice. "I affirm."

Then Gainor, his voice reluctant. "I affirm."

Then Desmond.

One by one, the councilors stood and affirmed the thane's decree, and my heart shattered a little bit more each time.

Last of all, Cormac stood.

Please. I held his gaze. *Please. You're a good man. I know you are.*

"I'm sorry, Kyla," he said. "I think you would be a wonderful mage. But we cannot overthrow the whole order for the whims of one person. We can't have a Phoenix who doesn't realize that. And you set a fire in your carelessness."

The last of my hope sputtered and died, like an extinguished flame.

"I affirm," said Cormac.

Dizziness. Disbelief. Uncontrollable heat burned behind my eyes. I whirled on my heel and stormed out of the tent so the council wouldn't see me cry.

THIRTY-ONE

How the blazes had everything fallen apart so quickly? An hour ago, I'd had the best practice of my life. I was on top of the world. I was . . . dancing with love. Whatever that even meant.

Blazes. Blazes. Blazes. Let the whole world burn.

I ran without stopping toward the glade. If Nolan wasn't there, I'd leave a note for him in the old oak. I wanted to see him. But more than anything, I couldn't stay in the camp. Couldn't face anyone else in the clan. Word would spread like a wildfire. I imagined talking to Breanna, Papa, Mama. The disappointment in their eyes.

Aislinn and Liam would quietly reassure me that it wasn't fair, but I didn't want to face their pity. Liam's obnoxious friends would just laugh at me.

The tears burned hot, but I held them back until I was beyond the edge of the festival. I wouldn't give them the satisfaction of seeing my agony. Not any of them.

I burst into the glen. Nolan was nowhere to be seen. I supposed he needed to go confess everything that had happened to his papa. To warn him to be on his guard, in case the council decided to move against him after all.

A note it was, then. But I realized I had no parchment to leave in the oak.

I slammed my fist against the wood. It sent pain racing through my arm, but I didn't care. I hit the tree again. And again. And again.

Then I sank down into the dirt and began to weep.

Everything was lost. I wasn't even a dancer anymore. I was nothing. My breath came in quick, short bursts.

The pain was too much. It overwhelmed me, weighed on my chest like it would crush me and leave my broken body lying there, battered, an empty husk.

I lay there, in the dirt, for hours. The sun began its descent, casting shadows in the fading lavender light, and the cicadas began their riotous song. But still I stayed where I was. Couldn't move. Couldn't think. Couldn't breathe.

At some point, the tears had stopped. I wasn't sure when. The pain had faded, too, leaving me numb. Maybe it really had killed me. Maybe this was what death felt like.

Still, I didn't move. I felt . . . paralyzed. Why wasn't I moving? It was time for me to go home.

But what was *home*, now?

The shadows had grown longer when I heard a voice. "Kyla?"

I pushed myself up to my elbows, my head tilting. *Papa?*

"Kyla!" the voice called again. Desperate. Afraid.

"Papa!" I called back, but my voice was weak, and I was sure it didn't carry far enough. I pushed myself to my knees.

Then Papa was running into the glen. "Kyla," he said again, his voice laced with relief. He ran to me and skidded to the ground, wrapping me in his arms. I sank into his warmth, letting it comfort me.

"Papa," I whispered, my voice breaking. The tears brimmed in my eyes again and then began to stream down my cheeks. "How did you find me?"

He didn't let me go. "Your uncle came to tell us what had happened. When you didn't come home, I went to the Malones' place to find you. Nolan was there, getting the lecture of his life from Dallan. I've never seen Dallan lose his temper like that. But Nolan told me where you'd probably be." He hesitated. "Why didn't you come home?"

My face crumpled. "I couldn't face everyone."

He held me tighter. "You scared me. I was afraid you had run away without saying goodbye. That you'd left without making a plan." He pulled back to look at me, and his eyes were red-rimmed. "Afraid you were out there alone. That someone would hurt you."

"I'm here, Papa," I whispered.

"I know." He stood and scooped me up like I was five years old again. "Let's get you back home."

When we arrived at the tent, Breanna and Mama were huddled around the table, and Darick was pacing the tent from end to end.

Breanna saw me first. "Thank the fire," she breathed.

"My baby!" Mama cried, her chair clattering backward onto the dirt as she stood and rushed toward Papa and me.

Papa set me on my feet, and Mama crushed me in a tight hug.

"Where were you?" she wailed.

Breanna joined us and rested her hands on both my shoulders.

"I didn't mean to frighten everyone," I said. "I just . . . needed time alone."

Mama squeezed me so hard I thought she might fracture my ribs. When she released me, Breanna took her turn, pulling me tight and whispering, "Don't scare us like that again, Kyla."

I wriggled out of their grasp and took a step back, wiping at my tearstained face. But the pity I expected to see in their eyes was missing. They just looked relieved.

My hands trembled. "I don't know what all Uncle Eamon told you. But I'm not a dancer anymore. My punishment for using magic." I stared straight at the ground, afraid of the judgment I would find in their countenances. I couldn't take judgment. Not today.

Breanna reached out and clasped my shoulder. "I'm just happy you're safe," she said.

Mama sniffled.

The numbness encased my heart again. "I'm sorry," I murmured, stepping to the side and heading toward the small tent flap that led into my room. "Sorry I disappointed you all."

Breanna moved to follow me. "Kyla—"

"I still need a little time alone," I said. "We'll talk about it tomorrow, Breanna. It's all still too fresh."

I met her eyes for a fraction of a moment, and she nodded at me. At that, I disappeared into my room and threw myself into the safety of my blankets. A bleak future unspooled itself in my mind. No dancing. No options but marriage. In less than a year, I was old enough for a formal betrothal. But who would marry me after such a scandal? After I'd been caught using magic and cast from the troupe? The humiliation smoldered in my chest. One of Liam's awful friends, maybe? The thought roiled my stomach.

I could stay unmarried, living in Mama and Papa's tent. The idea of the long years of *nothingness* stretching out before me was almost as horrifying as the idea of marriage to someone I loathed.

Or, I could leave the clan . . .

I could hear a stirring in the main area of the tent, and Breanna murmured, "Let's go, Darick. We'll let her sleep, and I'll come by tomorrow afternoon." She paused. "Nay, I have to go to the market tomorrow afternoon for fresh fruit. The warm weather is wilting all the produce. I'll bring Kyla back a bilafruit. Maybe a snail roll. I'll come for dinner."

Papa murmured his assent, and a few moments later, the tent flap swished, signifying that Breanna and Darick had gone. I burrowed deeper into my blankets and lost myself again in tears.

Early the next afternoon, I found Nolan sitting on our mossy rock. As soon as I saw his face, I burst into tears.

He jumped up and ran to me, enfolding me in an embrace. "Now we know," he said quietly.

"They . . . just took it from me," I sobbed against his chest. "All of them. Unanimous."

"Let's climb the tree," he said.

I nodded, but the misery still clung close to me from every side. With another heaving sob, I swung myself up into the tree and began to climb, trying to focus on the gentle burn in my muscles rather than on how everything was ruined.

Rather than on how very much I hated Shayla. Who was now the Phoenix. The *only* Phoenix. And I wasn't even a troupe dancer.

When I blinked, the white labyrinth intruded on my vision, but I shook it away. If I even thought about using magecraft in my current state, I might set the very world on fire.

We reached the familiar branches, as high as we could safely climb. That territorial squirrel chittered at me, scolding me for intruding on its territory, but I swatted at it, in no mood to humor it. Before I could make contact, it jumped up and scrambled further up the tree.

I settled into the groove in the branch, and Nolan eased into the vee beneath me. We sat there in agonized silence for a while.

And then I whispered, "Everything's ruined."

He sighed. "I'm sorry, Kyla."

"And I feel like such a fool. Who was I to think that they'd listen to me? That somehow I'd be the one to change the clan?"

More silence.

"Kyla," he said. "I . . . don't want to pressure you to make any decisions that you're not ready for. But yesterday . . . changes things, doesn't it?"

I wiped at my tears with my sleeve. "I know."

"The Fintan are leaving soon," he said. "In two or three weeks."

I didn't bother to reply. It was true. And I knew what he was about to say. I closed my eyes.

"I know you have a lot to think about. Your family. The new baby. Your whole world, really. But I want you to know that if it's time for you to leave the clan, you'll have a home with my family."

"Thank you," I managed through my tears.

"I'm not asking you to marry me or anything. I know there's a lot you want to do. I'm just saying that you'll have a place to stay, people who care about you."

"Aye." Wiping again at my tears, I turned the thought over in my mind. Reached into my bag to run my fingers over the coal. Over the marble. "I've a lot to think about," I said, my voice quavering. "But I might like that."

The more I considered the idea, the better it sounded. Stay with Nolan's family. Make friends outside the clan. Continue to learn magecraft without the oversight of the council. Maybe someday Nolan and I could travel. Go to the other side of the world, where the Fintan had never toured. Start up our own fire festival with a few other defectors, one where both men and women were mages and people could come and go as they pleased.

It was a sight better than marrying one of Liam's awful friends or staying in the clan and doing . . . nothing.

Pain still swelled in my chest, but some of the heaviness had lifted. Papa's words played in my head.

We're going to have to let her go someday.

Papa had known. Papa had always known. The tears returned with a vengeance, but it was a different sort of pain this time.

All wasn't lost. But oh, how it would hurt to say goodbye.

We sat there for an hour or so, until my tears subsided and left a dull ache in their place. "I'll stay," I said softly.

Nolan stirred beneath me. "I'm glad."

I managed a small smile. "It's the only thing left to do." Then I tilted my face up, sniffing. "Do you smell that?"

Nolan took a gulp of air, and his eyes widened. "Smoke," he said.

"But not woodsmoke."

He shook his head and smelled the air again. "No . . . it doesn't have the clean smell of woodsmoke."

Dread coiled in my stomach. Another fire? Could it be a coincidence? "Arson?" Wouldn't that just be the perfect ending to a perfect day?

The question hovered between us, dancing, flaunting all its horrifying possibilities. "Can you see where it's coming from?" he asked.

The flickering specter of arson tugged at me as I pushed myself to my feet, carefully gripping the branch above me for support. I scanned the forest in every direction. Nothing but leaves. "If I get just a little higher," I said.

"Be careful."

I hauled myself up onto the next branch. It swung beneath me, threatening to dump me off into the forest below. "Oh, no you don't," I murmured. If I stood from here, I was sure I could see above the other trees well enough to find the smoke. Inch by inch, I straightened, keeping my back against the trunk for stability.

There. In the distance, to the south. About where I'd expect . . .

"Terra Market," I said. A rush of horror flooded me, deeper

and stronger and blacker than the horror I'd felt while standing before the council being stripped of my role as Phoenix. My voice dropped to a hoarse, gravelly hiss. "Breanna was going there today. This afternoon." My sense of hearing faded away; my vision narrowed to a single point of light in a dark tunnel.

Breanna.

And then I was in the white maze, in front of a pillar I'd never seen before. Over the pillar was a surging flame that suddenly winked out of existence.

A voice whispered through the maze. This time, I could understand it. "There is still time to save her."

Breanna.

"I'm coming," I said as I jerked myself out of the maze and almost toppled off the branch.

"Kyla! Kyla!" Nolan called from two branches below me. "Are you okay? Please don't fall."

"We have to go now," I spat, swinging down to my usual branch.

"Do you think Breanna is still there?"

"The labyrinth thinks so." I jumped onto his branch and then down one further.

Nolan followed me down the tree.

"We have to go," I said again.

"What do you mean?" he gasped out from above me.

"I can put it out," I managed between gulps of air.

"Kyla, stop!" He dropped down next to me. "Your magic is too unpredictable. The quellers will deal with it."

"My sister is there!" I yelled. The branches were larger now, and I jumped from one to the next until I hit the ground and took off running toward the path.

I doubt I'd really convinced him it was a good idea, but he said nothing and ran alongside me. My breath was coming in hot, fast pants now. I hated running.

But I would not lose Breanna. I would die for her without hesitation or question.

Though I very much hoped it wouldn't come to that.

We reached the path and took off toward the south. I'd never run so fast for so long, but desperation fueled my every step. The pain in my lungs was nothing compared to the pain of burying Breanna and her child.

The Terra Market clearing opened up in front of us. Flames shot up from the old barn in the northwest corner, and a blaze was taking hold in another building somewhere toward the center. The road wound down the hill in a lazy serpentine, but we cut straight across the field. A horse galloped toward us, screaming in fear. The smell of smoke and seared flesh and burnt herbs filled my nostrils in a cacophonous, choking blend.

I dodged the horse and bolted toward the out-of-control blaze. The small wagon of three quellers was already here, but this fire was too much for them. They needed the rest of the quellers to have a hope of putting out a blaze this size. I looked around but didn't see any trace of the other two wagons.

Hurry up!

I hoped against hope that Breanna wasn't here, that she'd been in the open part of the market when the fire started.

But her favorite sellers set up shop in the stalls of the old barn.

I put on an extra burst of speed and arrived at the blazing wooden structure three steps before Nolan did. Grinding to a halt, I closed my eyes a moment and tried to focus.

Find Breanna, a voice whispered from deep in my soul. The same voice I'd heard in the labyrinth.

When I'd flashed into the labyrinth—back in the tree—the maze had shown me a tactic for extinguishing the fire. I was sure of it. I closed my eyes and entered the maze, finding myself standing on the smooth white floor before that same pillar. The fire flared to life in front of me in the shape of a phoenixbird, only to be instantly extinguished, leaving a bed of ashes in its stead.

"Tell me what to do," I hissed at the pillar. "I need to know. *Now*."

The whispering voice spoke in that strange language. But I had no time to try to interpret it. I needed to know how to put out the fire.

A louder, feminine voice spoke over the whispers. I'd heard that voice once before. "Do you love your sister?" the voice asked.

I whirled around, looking everywhere but finding no source for the voice. "Aye!" I yelled.

"Then you may take the flames that surround her into yourself," the voice intoned. "Leave the young man behind, or all will burn."

What the blazes is that supposed to mean? But the white room trembled, and a single crack appeared in the wall, snaking down toward the floor. Then there was a massive jolt, and I found myself back in the physical world, falling forward onto my face in front of Nolan.

Thud.

The fall knocked the air out of me, but I forced myself back to my feet before I fully caught my breath.

Horror flooded me as I looked up at the burning building. If the voice in the maze was right, Breanna was inside.

And I might be the only one who could save her.

THIRTY-TWO

I turned to Nolan. "Stay here," I said. "Promise me."

"What—"

"Promise me on your mama's soul. I don't have time to explain. The labyrinth spoke. You have to stay here or we all die." I whirled around and ran toward the burning barn.

"Kyla!"

The desperate, haunted timbre of Nolan's voice tugged at my heart as I bolted past three very confused quellers.

I'm sorry, Nolan. But I have to do this.

With every footstep, one of my failures flashed in my head. Steps I missed at dance practice. Times I'd disappointed Papa. The days I'd let the magic get out of control and started fires. And, worst of all, failing to convince the council. Watching them take away everything I'd worked for. I'd made so many mistakes. Lost so much.

None of that mattered now. I couldn't afford any mistakes here. I had to get to Breanna.

To Breanna's baby girl.

Overwhelming emotions swirled inside me as I ducked beneath the smoldering doorframe and into the blazing heat. I sucked in a breath of air, but only choking smoke filled my lungs. I pulled the collar of my shirt over my face and tried to suppress the hacking coughs. A high-pitched squeal met my ears, and I turned to see a small black cat bolt toward the entrance.

Where is Breanna?

I swallowed the bile rising in my throat and pressed deeper into the oppressive heat. When I blinked, I found myself for a moment in the labyrinth, staring at the pillar that had seemed to speak to me.

"Where is she?" I screamed.

I forced my eyes open. The orange flames leaped from rafter to rafter, casting an eerie, hellish glow over the whole scene. The fire crackled and hissed, spewing embers at me. I jumped forward, dodging a falling, flaming board that had torn free of the roof.

I tripped over something and tumbled to the ground, rolling across the fallen board and wincing as pain shot through my body. When I glanced back wildly to see what had tripped me, my heart broke in two pieces.

A little boy, perhaps five, his skin dark with soot, his brown hair sticking to his cheeks in damp curls. He was lying on the ground, his knees tucked into his chest. But his terrified eyes met mine. He was alive.

My gaze darted back toward the entrance. Where were the blasted quellers? I looked deeper into the burning barn. Why hadn't I let Nolan come with me? He could take the child to safety while I found my sister.

But the magic had spoken so clearly.

"Breanna, where are you?" I pleaded.

I lunged to my feet, scooped the boy into my arms, and bolted for the doorway, pleading with the fire to slow its murderous course.

A cracking sound tore the air, and I redoubled my pace. A burning beam came crashing down in front of me, and I didn't hesitate before I leaped over it and sailed through the door and out of the barn.

I sucked in a breath of life-giving air and bent over, coughing and hacking, trying to cleanse the choking smoke from my lungs.

"Kyla!" yelled Nolan.

I shoved the boy at him. "Take care of him," I rasped. "I have to get Breanna."

"She might not even be in there," he yelled.

"The labyrinth told me to." I held his gaze, my eyes pleading.

Nolan took the boy from my arms. "I'll go with you."

I shook my head. "Please, don't. The magic . . . told me. We'll die if you come. I can get her. I swear it." Then I sucked in a breath of air, turned, and fled back into the raging inferno.

The heat prickled across my skin, and then its full fury seemed to consume me. *Breanna!* I pushed into the barn, fear ravaging my very soul.

What if the voice is wrong? What if it's luring me into a trap?

I shook away the thought. If Breanna was here, I had to find her. I *had* to.

I leaped over the fallen beam and bolted into the depths of the barn.

Where is she? I demanded, hoping that the voice in the labyrinth could hear me. That it would give me an answer. Any answer.

Acid flooded my mouth when I saw a charred body off to my right. I refused to even think it could be Breanna.

But *someone* had lost their brother or sister to these flames. I pushed further into the barn, and something seemed to tug me to the left. I followed the instinct. Then I turned into a wide stall, and I saw her.

Breanna. On the ground.

I ran to her, bending over her, searching for signs of life. Relief flooded every inch of me when I saw her shallow breathing.

And then I noticed the others. Four children, hiding in the corner. Another woman, also unconscious.

The fire roared behind me. But maybe if the children dragged the other woman, I could shepherd them all out.

And then, the screaming of splintering wood. I whirled around just in time to see a post collapse behind me, and then a section of roof caved in, blocking our escape.

I turned back to the children, who stared at me with wide, panic-filled eyes.

We were trapped.

THIRTY-THREE

In that moment, my first thought was of Shayla. Of how satisfied she'd be that her nemesis was not only disgraced, but dead. Anger radiated out of my chest, and the flames flared even hotter, throwing more heat at my scalded skin.

I needed to focus. I needed to quell these flames, to carve a path through which I could drag Breanna and lead the children to safety. Or at least hold it off long enough for the quellers to rescue us.

Then a thin sheen of fire slithered its way across the ceiling, directly overhead. I swallowed. The quellers wouldn't reach us in time. We had to make it through the flames.

My eyes found the other unconscious woman—the children's mama, if the resemblance was anything to go on— and my throat burned. We would have to run. I could throw Breanna over my shoulder, but I couldn't rescue the woman too. If I tried to drag them both out, we'd all die.

I couldn't save everyone.

I whipped back around to stare at the flames that blocked our exit. "Come here," I called to the children.

I heard them shuffling behind me, and then one of the little ones wailed. "Ma-maaaa!"

My heart cracked. *Focus, Kyla.* I tried to steady myself. *Save Breanna. Save the children. Save . . .*

My vision flashed white. That confounded pillar pulsed in front of me like a living creature, underneath that uncanny symbol of fire pulling together and then exploding into nothing.

Of fire in the shape of a phoenixbird.

And then I understood the strange magic that the labyrinth had shown me. I'd been right.

I couldn't save everyone.

A child gripped my skirt, and I turned to look at her siblings, her mama, my sister.

But I can save all of the others.

I was still a phoenix.

Images of the life I'd dared to allow myself to dream of—a future with Nolan, first on his family's farm and then traveling in distant lands, forming our own festival—crowded at the edge of my thoughts, but I shoved them away.

No time to mourn that loss. No time to mourn my own life.

"Grab her," I called to the oldest two children, nodding at the unconscious woman. "Bring your mama over here." I gestured to Breanna. "Lay her beside my sister."

The children trembled but complied, their littler siblings sticking close at their sides.

The heat felt like it was going to melt my skin, and a pang of fear tugged on my heart at what I was about to do. But when I looked at the sweat trickling down Breanna's brow, I felt certain. This was why the labyrinth had welcomed me in, had spoken to me. It wasn't so I could pursue my own ambition.

It had known I would need to save them.

Breanna had been right. Love. It came down to love.

Because I was dancing for you.

"Huddle together with your mama," I called to the children.

I reached out with a tentative hand to squeeze my sister's fingers. And then I turned and faced the flames.

"You will not take them," I whispered. The world flashed white again, and I reached out and grabbed ahold of the pillar with both hands. When the white room faded and I found myself again in the fiery barn, I knew what to do. I stretched out both hands toward the fire.

I love you, Breanna.

And without a single word, I drew the flames toward myself. They came at me slowly, pulsing, as if surprised by my magic. Then hotter. Brighter. Tears burned in my eyes, but they evaporated before they could trail down my cheeks. Though I would be reduced to ashes, life would spring up from the blackened ground. Life for the children, for their mama, for Breanna and her baby.

The first wave of flame hit me, and I screamed. The searing-hot fire seemed to melt my skin and liquefy my bones, but I kept pulling, taking the fire into myself, until my whole body felt scorched from within. And still, I pulled the flames toward me, forcing myself to stay conscious through the pain with only the keen awareness of the love I had for my sister.

I'm sorry, Nolan.

I glanced back toward Breanna, and then threw out my hands and screamed into the inferno. All at once, the fire raced toward me like a living thing, engulfing me whole in brilliant white light.

THIRTY-FOUR

"Kyla!" Nolan's voice came to me as if through deep water. My mind swam, churning, trying to find the surface. Why was Nolan here? Had he run into the barn and died too? Had we stepped into the world beyond together?

"Kyla." Nolan again. Why wouldn't he let me sleep?

Awareness began to trickle through my being. The air was smoky. *How could I know that the air was smoky unless I was breathing?* The ground beneath me felt cool and gritty. I flexed my fingers and toes and experienced no pain. But something was different. A strange warmth pulsed inside me.

My eyes flew open.

Nolan knelt above me. People milled around the edges of my vision, speaking in hushed tones. Sunlight traced its tendrils over my body. I was alive. *But how?*

"Breanna," I managed, my voice hoarse. I lifted my hand and gazed at my fingers. They were dark, covered in soot. But whole, unburned.

How? But that wasn't the most important question.

"Breanna?" I said again, insistently.

"She's with Darick," Nolan said. "She's still unconscious. But she's breathing."

"And the baby?"

"Kyla, we don't know anything yet. Breanna looked . . . normal. A little sweaty? I'm sure the baby's fine."

I let myself relax into the ground. "What . . . happened?"

He let out a strangled laugh. "I should be asking you that."

With slow, tentative movements, I pushed myself up onto my elbows, searching for any sign of pain. There was none, but that heat inside me shifted with my movements. Like it was part of me. "What did you see?" I finally asked.

He hesitated. "The fire was getting worse. The quellers had surrounded the building and were trying to put it out, but it kept blazing hotter. As soon as they extinguished one area, the flames spread again. They couldn't keep up with it."

I nodded. That happened, sometimes, with bad fires. Even the quellers had their limits.

"And then all the flames . . . imploded. If that makes sense. And . . ." His eyes flinched with sudden pain.

"And what?" I asked gently.

"Enough of the barn had collapsed that I saw it happen," he whispered. "I saw *you*. The fire consumed you . . . I thought I'd lost you. And then . . . you consumed the fire."

I looked around. We were in what remained of the frame of the old barn. The building was partially collapsed and blackened, but not a live spark remained anywhere. I lay on a bed of ashes.

"The children?" I asked, my voice still hoarse. "And their mama?"

"They're fine," he said. "And the others, who were trapped in a different part of the barn. You saved twelve lives."

I sank back down into the ashes and closed my eyes. "I thought I was going to die," I murmured. "The labyrinth . . . showed me what to do. How to be a phoenix. To pull the fire into my own body to save the others." My eyes opened and searched out Nolan's. "But I thought it would kill me."

"It usually does," said a deep voice.

I sat up and whirled around. My uncle stood there with his arms crossed and a thoughtful look on his face.

I regarded him with curiosity, expecting anger to flash within me at the sight of him. But it didn't. I supposed after what had happened in the barn, my place in the troupe didn't seem quite as important as it had earlier.

Nolan took a step back, his face turning a shade paler. I pushed myself to my feet, standing between Nolan and the thane.

"What do you mean?" I asked.

"Do you know the story of the dragons?" asked my uncle.

I shifted, and ash crunched beneath my sandals. "The great beasts, or the ancient warriors?"

"The warriors," he said. "The beasts are pure legend."

"I thought the council said that the warriors were legend as well."

"The warriors have been naught but a story for a long time," he said.

"Powerful mages," I murmured. "Fire itself coursed through their veins."

"Mages with pure intentions, motivated by sacrificial care for others, who allowed themselves to be consumed by fire," he said. "Many mages tried to become dragons. Those who were tainted by greed or ambition were incinerated. A thousand years ago, the council decided we would no longer teach that magic."

I rubbed the back of my neck and tried to wrap my mind around what he was saying. But one thing I knew. "I'm nothing if not ambitious, Uncle."

He reached out and clasped my shoulder. "But you did not invite the fire inside you with ambitious intent. You did it to save the others, though you believed it would cost you your life. And the fire has deemed you worthy."

A shiver ran down my spine.

"You feel different, yes?"

That new heat surged in my chest. "Aye," I said. "Something has changed."

He nodded solemnly. "The fire has taken up residence inside you. It has become part of you, forever. No edict or council can change that. No matter how much we might wish it." He leaned more heavily against his staff. "You will appear before the council tomorrow so that we can all decide how we are to move on from here."

"Aye, Uncle," I said. My voice rang out strong and confident.

He turned and walked away, clicking his tongue. Before he strode out of earshot, I heard him mutter, "Most extraordinary, indeed."

"Kyla!"

I whirled around to see Papa running toward me. My chin quivered.

"Papa!" I darted forward and threw myself into his arms.

He held me close and brushed his lips against the top of my head. "Is it true? Did you run into that barn?"

Now the trembling overtook my whole body. "Breanna was in there," I whispered.

He stiffened, and when I drew back, his face was ashen.

"She's alive," I said. "Nolan said she's with Darick."

Papa pulled me tight against his chest again. "They said . . . they said you put out the fire."

I laughed, but it came out almost like a sob. "I did."

"They said . . ." He trailed off. "Nay, it is too strange."

This time, when I drew back, I looked him in the eyes. "It *was* strange, Papa. Uncle says I became a dragon-warrior. Like in the stories of the ancient days."

His eyes widened, almost imperceptibly. "Did you, now?" Even through his shock, I could detect a twinkle of pride. "Did you, now?"

I opened my hand, and a little ball of fire danced out of it. I looked down at it and then closed my hand. The flame vanished. It was effortless. Unlike all those hours practicing down by the old mill, I didn't have to strain to focus on the particles of fire. It just rolled out of me like . . . *like it's part of me.*

Because if the thane was right, it *was* part of me.

I looked up at Papa, and an awed smile spread across his face. "The first dragon in a thousand years, and it's my daughter," he said. "Now, isn't that something?"

Warmth spread in my chest, and it had nothing to do with the fire in my veins. "Let's go to Breanna."

THIRTY-FIVE

We found Breanna lying on a blanket stretched across the green grass. Darick knelt at her side, and two earth wizards—healers—were spreading ointment over her face, neck, and hands.

In the distance, I could still see the scorched-out barn. I dropped to my knees next to my sister. "Is she okay?" I asked Darick.

His face was as pale as sheep wool, but he managed a nod.

Breanna let out a little groan. "I can speak for myself." Her voice was faint, but I'd never felt so relieved to hear it.

"She's going to be just fine," said one of the healers, an older woman whose gray hair fell in a braid to her waist. "We're just putting this on her because of all that heat. Should alleviate any burns. Her lungs will take a few weeks to heal, but no reason she won't make a full recovery."

"The baby?" I asked.

The healer's expression was guarded. "It's too soon to tell. But nothing suggests she's miscarrying."

I could have broken down and wept right there.

Breanna opened her eyes and took me in. "You're covered in soot," she said. "Were . . . you in there too?"

I almost laughed, but I just said, "Aye."

"They said . . . something odd put out the fire," Breanna murmured, almost too quietly to hear.

Someday I'd tell her the whole story, but not yet. And not in front of anyone else. "Aye," I said. "It was curious."

"Go to sleep, Miss Breanna," cooed the younger of the healers. "You and the baby need a lot of rest."

"Mmm," she responded, her eyelids fluttering closed.

Darick squeezed Breanna's fingers more tightly, and I reached out and grabbed her other hand. He gave me a quizzical look, but I just shrugged and mouthed, "Not yet."

She needed to rest, not to marvel at what had happened.

We knelt in silence until Breanna's breaths rose and fell in a gentle, even rhythm.

The thane sat at the center of the long, rectangular council table. Blue fire blazed from a small cauldron in front of him, and the torches behind him flamed red. The other twelve council members also sat at the table, six on each side of the thane. And all of them were looking at Nolan and me.

But it felt nothing like before, when they had stared me down in judgment. Today, it felt . . . like they were afraid of me. Or maybe like they respected me.

Some of them, anyway.

A phoenixfly fluttered past me—behind me. But somehow, I knew, even though I couldn't see it. The fire in me could sense the phoenixfly's fire. I gripped Nolan's fingers tightly as I returned the thane's gaze. They had called me here to figure out what in the blazes they were going to do with me. But I was going to use this opportunity to plead Nolan's case again.

Especially because I had an inkling that all this *dragon* business gave me more negotiating power than I'd had a couple of days ago.

But I waited in silence. I'd let the thane speak first.

He studied me for another full minute before he said, "This is quite an extraordinary situation."

I tilted my chin up ever so slightly. The one small act of defiance I could allow myself. "So I hear."

He quirked his lips and then heaved a sigh. For the first time, I noticed the white hairs sprinkled throughout his red hair. Saw the tight lines of worry on his face. His responsibility weighed on him. Had aged him.

I hadn't seen it before.

Niall Hannigan, two seats down from the thane, leaned forward, his hands pressed together. "So, you fancy yourself a dragon, now?" Mirth tugged on the corners of his lips.

Condescending beetle.

About half the council chuckled to themselves. I waited for the anger, hot and searing, to flare up in me . . . but it didn't. The obnoxious, puffed-up men who were mocking me just seemed . . . small. They thought themselves kings of the world, but they didn't know how wide and mysterious the world was.

"I *am* a dragon," I said, squeezing Nolan's hand again.

"And I'm a flaming unicorn," crowed Niall.

Now that *did* provoke a flash of irritation in me.

"Did you learn nothing from our ruling?" Niall demanded. "Girls can't be mages, much less dragons. And there hasn't been a dragon in a millennium. If they ever existed at all. You wouldn't have the first idea how to do that magic, heifer."

This time the anger surged in my chest. I'd always loathed that man.

The thane held up his hand, but Niall kept going.

"You're trying to usurp authority over the men of—"

The blue fire in front of the thane pulsed into a tower of flame, reaching almost to the top of the tent. *Effortless.*

Niall sputtered and looked from me to Nolan. He raised a trembling finger and pointed at Nolan. "I see through your cheap parlor trick. Was it really Kyla who extinguished the torches when you were on trial? Or have you been doing it all for her?"

"Niall," the thane's voice boomed deep. "You shame yourself and this council."

Niall's face flushed, and he opened and closed his mouth before falling silent.

Cormac Flynn stood, and in that moment, he looked just like Liam. He'd always been kind to me, his vote at the previous meeting notwithstanding. I relaxed.

"But . . . we need proof, don't we?" Cormac asked, his voice hesitant. "No offense, Miss Kyla. I've never known you to tell a lie. It's just . . . there's no question something strange happened down at the market. Each story is wilder than the last. But the return of dragon magic? It hasn't been seen in generations. How do we know that this . . . phenomenon you've observed is really dragon-warrior magic?"

I swallowed. Another phoenixfly floated above my head. It had come down through the hole where smoke vented from the tent, I supposed. Odd. Phoenixflies didn't usually come inside.

"I don't," I said. "All I know of the ancient dragons is what our great thane told me after I awoke from the fire— and what my mama told me in bedtime stories when I was small. But I have no better explanation." Even now, my blood felt hot, like fire and blood intermingled in my veins in a mystical dance. We always said that the Fintan had fire in our blood . . . but it was an expression. A figure of speech. It wasn't like this.

Then I let the fire rise up and out of me, until it was dancing on my skin.

Nolan gasped and dropped my hand. I looked down at my arm, and the sight took my breath away.

Fire stretched out across my body in a thin layer, pulsing like a living thing. *Well done,* said a voice in my mind. I tilted my head. I knew that voice.

It was the voice that had spoken to me from inside the labyrinth. Now it was inside me.

Illuminate, said the voice.

The fire rose off me in a perfect halo around my body.

Call it back, said the voice.

It barely took a conscious thought, and the fire contracted, tingled on my skin for a moment, and vanished. I felt a warming sensation as it eased back into my veins.

I held Niall's astonished gaze and then nodded at Cormac. "Does that settle the matter?" I asked quietly.

By the looks on their faces, I knew I'd proved it. Beyond any doubt.

Though the thane still seemed perturbed, a smile spread across his face. Perhaps he enjoyed Niall's humiliation as much as I did.

"As I said," intoned the thane, "this is quite an extraordinary situation."

Niall slammed his fist on the table. "She's a girl. She can't learn magecraft."

Cormac called, "I'd say she already knows magecraft better than you do."

Niall shot to his feet. "How dare—"

Nolan and I rolled our eyes at each other as those at the table devolved into a heated squabble.

"Order!" called the thane over the commotion. "I demand order!"

The raucous voices calmed.

"Now," said the thane, adjusting the collar of his robe. "Kyla is a dragon. That much is clear. So we must discuss, in a calm, civilized manner, how we will proceed."

Niall said, "I—"

The thane cut him off. "I believe you've already contributed your opinion to the council."

Niall's face turned an even brighter shade of red, if such a thing were possible.

"Don't see as we have much of a choice," piped up Desmond, who sat beside the thane. "It's not like she just knows a few tricks. Two days ago, she told us we had no choice but to train her, but she was wrong then. She didn't know so much that she could force our hands. But now? There's a power inside her that most of us barely plumb in our whole lives. But she's very young. She still has a lot to learn." He turned to look at me, running a hand through his beard. Then he nodded, as if offering a begrudging respect. "And I reckon she has a lot to teach us."

The council members nodded, except for Niall and Old Rory.

That might be as good as it gets. I stepped forward. "On one condition," I said.

This time even the thane scoffed at me. "You think you have a right to dictate your terms to us?"

A phoenixfly alighted on my shoulder, and its brilliant purple flame changed to a vibrant red.

"I don't know about the *right* to dictate anything," I said, "but I know I do have the right to leave the Fintan behind and make my own way in the world."

The thane's jaw tightened.

"And if you try to stop me"—my voice intensified— "maybe you'd succeed. If all of you worked together. But I think the damage would make that barn fire look like a cooking pit."

The thane drummed his fingers on the table. "Proceed."

I took a deep breath. "The council is right that I still have a lot to learn. I need to be sure that I can control this magecraft, that I know how best to use it for the good of the clan. I need to practice, and I need to learn the history of the dragon-warriors. All of the ancient stories. Everything we know. So these are my conditions: I am given the freedom to pursue mage training, learn everything I need to know, and pursue the use of this gift, just as any man would have."

The thane nodded. "That seems reasonable, under these unusual circumstances."

"And Nolan," I continued. "Nolan is to be trained as a mage and welcomed back into the community. His family, too, if they want."

This time, the thane shook his head. "We've discussed this, Kyla. You know that is in violation of our strictest laws."

"I don't care," I said through gritted teeth. "You can agree, or you can say goodbye to me and to the magic inside me."

The thane leaned back in his seat and studied me, as if trying to gauge how serious I was. "Alright, then," he said. "The boy can train, as can any of his brothers who show evidence of the elemental fire. And his sister may join the clan as well. But not his papa."

My head snapped up.

The thane's eyes burned. "The boy and his siblings had no choice in the circumstances of their birth, and we are nothing if not forgiving and merciful."

I suppressed a snort.

"But his papa chose to leave us—to reject the community that raised him, to go off with a woman from outside the clan. He has made his choice."

Swallowing, I glanced at Nolan. He nodded. And even though part of me wanted to stand my ground and demand that the council agree to each and every demand, I sensed a rigid core in the thane's words.

And Nolan's papa *did* leave.

"That will be fine," I said.

The thane nodded solemnly. "I'm glad to hear it. Any other demands?"

Let all the girls be mages? The answer rose up in me unbidden, but I sequestered it, locking it away in a tiny corner of my heart. Someday soon, I'd unleash that desire and fight for thoroughgoing change. Today, I would choose which wars to wage.

A phoenixfly landed on my shoulder, and its heat mixed and melded with mine. "That's it," I said.

"You may go," said the thane with a curt nod of his head.

I whirled around and hazarded a glance at Nolan as we walked away, ducking through the tent flap and heading toward the encampment.

"I can't believe it," he said when we reached my tent.

A smile turned up the corner of my mouth. "We did it," I whispered.

He turned to face me and tucked a strand of my hair behind my ear. "*You* did it."

I bit my lip and glanced down at the ground. An extinguished phoenixfly was walking toward me on its six tiny legs. I reached down to touch it, and it blazed to life in red flames as soon as my hand brushed its wings. "Everything's going to be different now, isn't it?" I stood back up, and my eyes searched Nolan's.

"Aye," he said. "In the best of ways."

THIRTY-SIX

"Breanna?" I called as I approached her small white tent. The grass under my feet felt cold—most things had felt cold since the flames took up residence inside my veins. Like I'd become warmer than the rest of the world. I wondered if I'd get used to it in time, or if it would feel that way until my last breath.

"Come in!" Darick called from inside the tent.

I ducked through the thin fabric and nodded at Darick.

He wore an apologetic expression on his face. "I told her about the . . . dragon business," he said. "I shouldn't have. It's your story. But she was asking questions and—"

"It's okay," I said. "Don't worry about it. I've had to tell the story twenty times today, it feels like." I took in my sister lying on the sleeping mat on the far side of the one-room tent, and tears welled in my eyes.

"Breanna!" I swept to her side and knelt beside her.

Her eyelashes fluttered open. "Hey, there," she said. Her voice sounded dry and cracked, but that didn't stop the sparkle in her eyes.

"Are you feeling better?" I asked.

She started to speak, and then a fit of coughs overtook her body. A moment later, Darick appeared at my side, a cup of water in his hand. He offered it to Breanna, and she took a long sip.

When she was able to breathe again, she said, "I felt the baby move."

This time, the tears spilled down my cheeks. The baby

was okay. New life had indeed arisen out of the ashes. And I was alive to see it. Gratitude overwhelmed me.

I swallowed back the swell of emotion. "You know, she'll be the most spoiled child in Fintan history if her Auntie Kyla has anything to do with it."

"So you've said." She chuckled, a wry smile on her chapped lips. Then her expression grew serious. "There's no one else I'd rather she look up to."

I shifted, reaching out to clasp her hand. "I learned it all from you."

"Then you learned it better than I ever did."

Shaking my head, I said, "Nay, Breanna. You love fiercely. Way better than I do. I'm ambitious and proud and self-centered so much of the time. But you? You've never been like that." I looked down at the ground. "You loved me better than you loved yourself, even when we were children. You showed me how to harness the fire's power."

A single tear slipped down her cheek, and then the dam broke in my chest. My tears streamed freely.

Breanna cried, too, and when she pushed herself to a seated position, we held each other, our tears mingling in our hair until the emotion faded to embers.

"I'm so proud of you," Breanna whispered. "But promise me one thing, Kyla."

"Anything."

"For now, you need to learn. Learn everything that they wouldn't let you learn because you were born a girl." She sat up, her back perfectly straight, and rested a hand on her abdomen. "Because now you wield a power that the rest of us can only guess at."

I nodded, though I still couldn't wrap my mind around any of it.

"Promise me that my daughter will have options that you and I weren't given. From a young age. By the time she's seven and starting her lessons."

By the time she's seven.

I clasped Breanna's forearm. "I swear it." This time, it was my voice that was hoarse.

"But"—she pulled away and lay back down on the mat, and her voice grew stronger—"I suspect you'll have a lot to do between now and then. Darick said the quellers confirmed that the market fire was arson."

The hair on my arms stood up. "The arsonist left signs this time?"

"Maybe he was in a hurry," she said. "The market is so busy. It'd be hard to set a blaze without being seen."

I mulled that over.

"Darick said you were meeting with the thane?" she asked. "What did he want with you? Did he talk about the arsonist?"

I shook my head. "Nay. It was a brief conversation. Mostly I proved to the whole council that I'm a . . . *dragon.* And then I made them let Nolan and his siblings into the clan."

"Wonderful news." Breanna's eyes gleamed. "Remember, you're our greatest weapon now, if half the stories of the dragon-warriors are true. The council has to find the arsonist. They might well need you for that. They'll need you for so many things. To protect the people. Don't let them dismiss you or belittle you. Because you know they'll try."

I rolled my eyes. "They certainly tried at the council meeting today."

She sighed. "It will be hard for them to get used to you. But they will. In time." Her lashes drooped closed again. "I'm sorry. I'm . . . very tired. The healers said I need rest."

I bent over and kissed her forehead. "Sleep, Breanna. You'll be on your feet again soon."

I nodded at Darick as I stood and strode to the tent flap. When I looked back, he was tucking the blankets around Breanna's feet.

A small smile spread across my face.

I ducked through the opening and out into the encampment. Breanna's words ran through my mind.

You're our greatest weapon now. Did the thane want to talk to you about the arsonist?

I scanned the horizon for telltale smoke, but the sun shone in a brilliant blue sky untainted by clouds or any hint of fire.

A swarm of phoenixflies in brilliant flames of amethyst and crimson and every shade of blue swooped out of the sky toward me—they seemed to be attracted to my fire these days—and, all at once, they landed in my hair and on my shoulders. When they touched me, their wings blazed red.

To protect the people, Breanna had said.

I'd been given this gift, this bond with the fire, because I'd surrendered my life to save my sister and everyone else in that barn. Part of me *had* died in the blaze. Because my life, as I'd always known it, was over. The fire had spared me. And I would not fail it.

I held my head high. *Aye, Breanna. I will protect the people, as best I can.*

No matter the cost.

A NOTE FROM THE AUTHOR

Did you like the book? I'll be forever grateful if you take the time to leave a review on Amazon, Goodreads, or Barnes and Noble. Reviews are the #1 way you can help other people discover the authors you love, and each and every review supports us on our journey to bring you more stories. A review doesn't have to be long or detailed—just honest! I'm so thankful for each and every one of you.

Burn bright!

KYLA'S STORY WILL CONTINUE IN . . .

FIRE MAGE

MAGIC IS A VOLATILE POWER.

Kyla is the first girl in the history of the fire festival to be trained as a mage. But there's still so much she has to learn. As she continues to explore and refine her incredible power, a simmering threat erupts: the Orivesi arsonist has struck again, and powerful families are aligning themselves against the fire festival.

As Kyla struggles to maintain control over her magic in order to help calm the inferno, heartbreak stalks her every step. For the council is deadly serious about maintaining exclusive control on the practice of fire magic, even if it means a massacre. And the day is coming when everyone must choose a side.

ACKNOWLEDGMENTS

Novel writing is a team sport, and I'm so grateful for the people who have gotten me to the finish line on this one.

First and utmost, to Jesus, who sustains me.

Thanks to my production team. This book would have been a mess without each and every one of you:

My editors: Lindsay Franklin, Stephanie Monk Guido, S.D. Grimm. You're all brilliant.

My cover artist: Jenny Zemanek at Seedlings. You always do such beautiful work, but I gasped aloud when I saw the final version of this cover.

My formatters, Chris Bell at Atthis Arts and Kella Campbell at E-Books Done Right. Your eye for detail is above and beyond.

Thanks to the dancers who critiqued my dance scenes: Sabrina Ramoth, Kelli Dowling, Denica McCall, and Julia Evans.

To my Wonder Women: Avily, Lindsay, Sarah. I love you guys. Thanks for being my people.

To other friends, especially Chris, Stephanie, Jessica, Rainey, and Lizzy.

And finally, to my ever-supportive husband and family. Brendan, always. Mom, you're my biggest fan and have always modeled strength. Nancy, you're the best mom-in-law a girl could ask for. Phil, your academic research means the world to me and helped me give voice to the themes of this book. Carly, Claire, Ava, Miriam, Eliana, Annaliese, Madison, and Naomi: you're the reason I write about girls who pursue life with everything in them and don't apologize for taking up space. Benjamin, Caleb, Timothy, Nathanael, Jonathan H., Jonathan P., and Ethan: these stories are for you, too, as you grow into men like Kyla's father. Brittany, you are my Breanna. Ted, I used to think you stole my big sister, but I actually just gained a pretty awesome older brother that day. Jason, I'm glad we talk about life these days. Stacey, our family has never deserved you. Angel, I cherish our heart-to-hearts.